Escape into the Reverie

A short story collection

by Heather Wilson

ISBN
Paperback 979-8-9921401-0-1
Hardbback 979-8-9921401-1-8
eBook 979-8-9921401-2-5

Cover design by GetCovers
https://getcovers.com/

Edited by Heather Wilson

Acknowledgements

To Mom, Dad, Vance, Chris, and Natassia, who have supported me through my education and through me working to publish this book (albeit unsuspecting of my intentions to publish a book).

To the niece of my dreams, Mila, who brings joy to my life every single day.

To Theresa, Celeste, Eric, Manuel, Makenna, Lauren, Basil, Elluka, Adrianna, Izzy, Sapphire, Ky, and Kyra, whether for our adventures together or your willingness to review my writing for me and to offer earnest feedback (again, albeit unsuspecting of my intentions to publish a book).

And to you, the one reading this book, for choosing to *Escape into the Reverie.*

Table of Contents

Beloved from Beyond..5

Karma.. 21

The World is Ours...40

Reunited...46

The Lake Nymph... 58

Recital of Roses.. 84

Forest of Fantasy.. 110

Beloved from Beyond

We were meant to be together forever. Coraleigh was the best thing that ever happened to me. At our engagement party, we were surrounded by all of our loved ones. Friends and family all were there to give us their well wishes, family especially. Coraleigh's immediate family always spared no expense when it came to spoiling her and making her feel special, regardless of what she was celebrating. It was an honor, knowing that I would get to marry into this family; to say she was loved would be an appalling understatement. All while she was given the love and luxury she deserved, she never believed herself entitled to it, and it only made me wish to maintain the lifestyle her family had thoroughly accustomed her to, to ensure that she would never want for anything so long as I had a say in it.

This, I vowed in advance in hopes of being a worthy husband to her.

Coraleigh donned a long lavender dress, her makeup having been done up to magnificence by her friends earlier so that she would be ready when I proposed. The warmer tones brought out her eyes by contrasting them, yet they matched her personality. Likewise, her nails were done as well; classic French tips. Her hair was curled, though it softened into waves over the course of our day out. Still, she maintained a perfection about her. That, or my own view of her was perfect; she fretted over the slightest thing in her appearance. She wanted to look her best for me, and I appreciated every effort. I couldn't tell if I loved her so much that I overlooked her flaws or adored them all the same.

In front of everyone, I held her hands. They always were so soft, and I was equally proud to hold those same hands in private, away from everyone's prying eyes, as I was publically. I met her gaze, and while I paid little mind to everyone around us, I felt their love and support radiating onto us. I was on top of the world. The love of my life stood before me, and I would have married her right there and then if I could. But our marriage needed to be planned; someone like Coraleigh needed something special, something that was not haphazardly thrown together.

"You have made me the happiest man alive." I told her. "I already know that today is only the second best day of my life; the best will be the day we say 'I do'."

"Cory," Coraleigh spoke, "I will always–"

At that moment, her eyes widened, and she began to bleed. A gunshot sounded, and none of us had adequate time to process what happened. As horrified gasps and screams filled the room, I turned my attention to the gunman. The gunman who single handedly took every reason worth living away from me, all in an instant. Why would he do this? Why would he do something to make me so miserable?

My attention was directed to Coraleigh, who cupped my cheek and turned me to face her. "Cora, baby, everything will be okay–"

"Cory…" She repeated. "Cory, I…"

"Shhh, we're going to get you looked at as soon as possible." I reassured her, even if it was mostly to reassure myself. I stroked her hair, hoping that it comforted her; it did little to comfort me, but I needed desperately to do it.

"Co… ry…" Was the last utterance of my darling Coraleigh. The look on her face suggested that she was not ready to die. I was not ready for her to die either. Her mother and her cousins surrounded us, as if hoping they could somehow bring her back. If I could have, I would have done it myself.

Anger surged through me; there needed to be justice for Coraleigh. Her brother, my brothers, and her male cousins were quick to catch the gunman, and her father beat him ruthlessly. It truly was mercy that the cops arrived when they did; we all thought that he would beat him to death. We *hoped* that sorry excuse of a man would be beaten to death. I should have partaken in holding him down and assisting Coraleigh's family. Had I not been holding onto the corpse of my beloved, I would have gladly joined them. Her body was a weight which kept me held back from resorting to utter violence; Coraleigh herself would not have wanted me to behave animalistically. That was what I tried to assure myself of, anyway. Hesitantly, I closed her gorgeous eyes for her. My tears ran down my cheeks, as it served as confirmation that she was really gone, that those bright eyes I cherished looking into would never open again.

Guilt coursed through my veins. I should have done *more* for her, and I could not sate this need for the life of me. Even when I ardently advocated that the gunman get the death penalty for his crimes against Coraleigh, against our families who should have been united with our matrimony but are united due to tragedy, against *me.* I showed my face proudly in court, in spite of my shock at Coraleigh's death leaving me too paralyzed to act sufficiently. I stared the gunman in the face, not caring in the slightest what weak defense his lawyer had for his mental state at the time of the attack. There was a pride about him which I wanted to extinguish, just like he had extinguished my sweet fiancée's life. I hated everything about him, including but not limited to that stupid look on his face. Who was he to smirk about what he had done?

"You couldn't save her." He uttered. I could have sworn I heard him taunting me; he wanted me to react, to completely throw the case that her family and I were sure to win.

Had I not been the gentleman that Coraleigh fell for, had I not had any reason to keep myself composed, I would have lunged at him and pummeled him into the ground. However, I had to be strong; Coraleigh needed justice, and I could not act too brashly, or I would jeopardize that justice. At least, that was how I had to think; even if the case was clearly easy for us to win, it was not easy for any of us to get through.

I thought I would be more satisfied when the court had sentenced the gunman to the death penalty that I so ardently advocated for. Don't get me wrong, the justice system worked quite well in that case, yet the feeling of loss still gripped my heart horrendously. It gripped me the way Coraleigh grabbed onto my shirt, as if to desperately cling on for dear life. I was what she needed, yet I was not enough to sustain her long enough to get her seen by a doctor and to have her healed. My presence was not enough to see her through to our wedding, and as a result I got to witness her funeral that should not have taken place for many, many years. It pained me to have to throw it together so quickly. I only agreed to her family's wishes, not wanting to make anything more difficult than it had to be; she would not want tension and arguments to break out as a result of her passing. Coraleigh disliked all forms of chaos, and I would not stand for it at an event meant to commemorate her life.

Her sister, Colette, held onto me at the funeral, sobbing profusely at the notion of having to bury her older sister too early. We sought each other out for comfort, and as a result, we kindled a love between us. In a strange way, it felt healing to the both of us, even if it gave me all the more reason to allow the rest of the family to make decisions in regard to the planning of the funeral. She looked so much like her sister, and I could not help but to succumb to the inviting temptation of her comfort. I always believed that nobody would measure up to Coraleigh, that I could not see myself with someone different from her; who better than her sister, who closely resembled her and loved and cherished her as I did? Her blonde hair was the same shade, and sure, it would take getting used to, to look into bluish green eyes instead of blue eyes, but already we found each other in love. Colette always loved the way I treated her sister, always remarking that she wished she had a relationship like ours. As much as I assured her that she would one day find someone to treat her well, the opportunity had presented itself through the tragic loss of Coraleigh. We justified this by implying that Coraleigh would want the both of us to be happy. The disapproval of her family did not exactly help us, though I knew to understand how they felt. Hopefully, though, they would come to understand and even accept our feelings, as well as the blossoming relationship that resulted from the tragedy. After all of our suffering, we needed something positive to look forward to. However, I could not shake a particular guilt that hung about me; I grew self conscious as I considered what Coraleigh might have thought of this.

The weather on the day of the funeral was fitting; the sky raged with rain and thunder. Many of us cried angry tears at the injustice of her life ending so soon, myself included. The just death of the gunman brought us no justice, and it certainly did not bring Coraleigh back to life, no matter how much we wished it would. I felt the judgmental stares of her parents as I held onto Colette and tried to comfort her. Perhaps we had made our newfound relationship known too soon; Colette *did* want to wait until after the funeral. Unfortunately, however, we had been caught; Colette and Coraleigh's sister Cordelia overheard us, and she laid into us as to what shame we brought upon the family by being together so soon after Coraleigh's death. With some choice words, she suggested that perhaps we went as far as to sneak off together while Coraleigh was still alive, that we were waiting for an excuse to be together. Of course, Cordelia told the rest of the family, and they all knew just in time to pass judgment on us at the funeral.

As they began to walk away, Colette and I approached the open casket. We knew it would be time for her to be buried soon, and this was our chance to say goodbye to her one last time. Colette looked at me with a frown.

"Cory," she said, "are you sure we're doing the right thing? I mean… It's so soon. I… I feel like I stole you from my big sister."

"Nonsense," I assured her, "the only thing you've stolen me from is grief. As harsh as it is, we have no chance of Coraleigh ever coming back. I would be planning my wedding with her right now if it weren't for the murder. Fate has strange ways of bringing people together; Cora would tell you that herself. Besides, Cora would want us to be happy, even if it meant seeking that happiness out in each other."

We whispered to each other; we knew that the family had not taken kindly to our relationship. It would take time for them to heal, too, and especially to warm up to the idea of Colette and me, in place of Coraleigh and me. I swore their judgmental stares seeped into me, and I did my best to ignore it. Simultaneously, we were mourning and we were harshly condemned for the way we chose to cope with our grief.

As we watched Coraleigh, she looked peaceful. It was a shame that she had to die in the same dress she got engaged in. The dress she was supposed to wear as the beginning of her happily ever after turned into the dress she wore in her casket. I could not bear the thought of burying her, and neither could her family. In fact, I believed that not even the earth was ready to hide her inside of it forever. I reached inside, stroking her cheek while holding an umbrella over the three of us. Myself, her little sister, and her. I sighed, tears filling my eyes once more. Colette patted my back gently, reminding me of her loving presence as I grieved for my lost love. I leaned in to kiss Coraleigh on her forehead, and at that moment, thunder struck the earth. I thought the screams coming from her family were due to the thunder. Colette screaming and pointing at the casket, however, told me it was something else.

Coraleigh's eyes opened. She stared at us, her pale face having been done up with makeup for the funeral. The only color was in the blush on her cheeks, as opposed to her normal rosy complexion which was so vibrant and alive.

"Co… ry…" Coraleigh spoke, surprising me. I backed away nervously when she sat up in her casket. "Cory…"

Her family fled, shrieking in terror. Coraleigh was miraculously reanimated, yet none of us knew her intentions. Immediately, however, we assumed the worst; perhaps Colette's doubts were reasonable after all.

Coraleigh might have been displeased to see that I got together with her younger sister. We all knew each other in high school, and I knew age in and of itself was not the issue. I was meant to be Coraleigh's, though, and I quickly turned to her sister after her death.

"Cory." Coraleigh called out as she climbed out of the casket. Her long dress was tattered at the ends as it tore with her climbing out, yet this did not stop her. If anything, it was all in her way, and despite the obstacles, she would stop at nothing to come after me. Her voice, which sounded so sweet, now had a haunting lilt to it. A deathly dulcet droned in place of the lively, lovely cadence that all who knew her were well accustomed to.

As Colette beheld her sister, she screamed, and I grabbed her by the hand.

"Come on!" I shouted as I took off running, bringing her with me. Who knew what revenge Coraleigh would want to inflict upon us? Coraleigh walked briskly; her muscles had no chance to deteriorate, yet she had not used them for about a week. As clumsy as her movement was, she clearly could rely on her muscle memory to keep her moving and to muscle through the stiffness. Everything happened too fast for me to process it, and now we were being chased down by her.

We ran across the bridge over the river. It was a lovely bridge; I intended to have wedding photos taken on that bridge with Coraleigh. Here I should have joyfully swung her around or lifted her into the air, or any pose she wanted for pictures for that matter. We now fled in terror from her instead. She should have been in her wedding dress, surrounded by loved ones and given attention and affection. The pleasant smile, the perfectly coiffed hair, and her makeup should have been done to perfection.

The reality contrasting the unattainable day of my dreams reminded me how cruel fate was to my beloved Coraleigh. There was obsession in her eyes, as she was on a mission. I did not want to stick around to see what it was, or what she was capable of. As cowardly as that was of me, and as much as I knew I deserved to meet such a fate for failing to save her and for pursuing her younger sister promptly after her untimely death, I trembled to think of what she might do to me. Her dress continued to tear as it snagged onto old wooden posts and onto chipped metal railings, yet it remained long and pooled behind her in all of its tattered glory. Her hair was messy, like she just woke up from a nap. A nap after a party, that is; her hair was styled for the funeral, as if to preserve the glow about her from the day of the engagement party. I saw her wake up from post party naps, and that dazzling smile always shined through even the sleepiest of her stupors. Even when her makeup was smudged, like it was now from the rain pouring down and ruining the image of still perfection, she was glorious. Hauntingly beautiful. Not that I could spend a moment to appreciate it; I could only assume that she was a woman scorned, one that hell's fury could not compare to.

As much as she fussed over her appearance, she cared so little for it now; she only continued in her pursuit of me, leaving Colette and me breathless. We couldn't stop for rest; Coraleigh wouldn't stop.

"Cory…"

"Don't slow down!" I shouted at Colette, concerned about the ire she might want to take out on her younger sister.

"Cory, she wants *you!*" Colette protested breathlessly.

"*Cory…*"

I could have sworn she was gaining on us. How was this possible? I was always faster than her! There was determination in her voice; even as she was getting used to speaking again, she insisted on using every ounce of her being to hunt me down.

Colette and I found an old, abandoned barn, slipping inside to hide from Coraleigh. We hoped we lost her, shutting the doors behind us. There were holes in the walls; this barn had been long abandoned, never to be cared for again and practically waiting to fall apart. The thought occurred to me that we could have been crushed inside of it, and it only sent my anxiety through the shoddy roof which barely protected us from the heavy downpour of rain.

"Cory, what if she finds us?" Colette panicked in a hushed voice.

"There's a pile of hay." I pointed out. "*Hide.*"

"But it's right next to the door–" Colette attempted to protest.

"I mean it, get in there and hide." I told her.

"What about you–"

"*Hide!*" I warned her through gritted teeth, too fearful of what consequences she may face should Coraleigh see her.

Beside the door was a rack full of various tools, all of which rusted over from years of abandonment and water damage. As Colette hid herself inside the hay pile, which ended up being more limited than we originally thought, she moved toward the tool rack, wanting to make the tools all the more available to her. She reached for the pitchfork, her hand shaking. I never wanted her to attack her sister with farming tools. In fact, I put my hand up, as if to prepare to tell her to keep her hands off of the tools and to keep her from coming after Coraleigh. At that moment, however, the barn doors opened; there stood Coraleigh.

As Colette trembled, her grasp on the pitchfork tightened, and she stared her sister down. As soon as Coraleigh glanced her way, that boldness died on the spot; Colette dropped the pitchfork, the clattering startling not only Coraleigh but also me. Evidently, however, Coraleigh did not wish to take any of her wrath out on her sister. She only looked for me, and she quickly found me; the effort to hide myself was insufficient.

"Cory." The walking corpse made its way toward me. I stood still, now accepting my fate; I deserved punishment, especially because I dragged poor Colette along with me for the ride. Perhaps Coraleigh and I were meant to go to the grave together, even if it were not in the way I originally imagined.

Several steps into the barn, and lightning struck the rooftop. The ceiling fell upon Coraleigh, crushing her underneath it. Colette gasped, covering her face like she knew she was somehow in trouble for allowing this to happen.

Guilt overtook my senses; I could not allow Coraleigh to remain crushed underneath the large chunks of wood. I lifted it off of her, tossing the wood aside to reveal her lying on the ground. Upon seeing me, she reached up, like she had the day we lost her.

"Cory." Coraleigh said, an insistent pleading to her tone. Her gaze significantly softened from the crazed look she donned earlier.

"Cora, I'm here, baby." I told her as I supported her; there could have been hope for us after all. We could have had the life that we were supposed to all along. "I'm so sorry. Colette and I, I know it was rushed, we just missed you so much and we couldn't take it…"

"... I just wanted to tell you…" Coraleigh clutched onto my shirt once more. "... I will always love you…"

At that moment, her tight grip loosened, and she left her body once more, lying limply in my arms as my hope left with her.

Karma

Because there had to be some good in the universe, there had to be some sort of restorative justice. I knew that if everyone got away with all of the cruddy stuff that they did, that there would be no incentive to do good or to refrain from the bad. Everybody had their personal reasons to hope in such a thing, myself included.

I was a good person. This, I was more than certain of. Everyone else in my circle thought so, going as far as to shower me with praise for it. I mean, I certainly tried to keep it that way. That way, I would stand out from everyone else who wanted their enemies to get their comeuppance. I had to stand out among the rest.

I had heard of the things that Karma could do to people. Because of this, I saved it for a particular moment. I waited for someone to do me especially wrong before I would try to seek it out. For the time being, however, I did my own dirty work in getting people back. It would only make things harder for Karma, and surely Karma had enough to deal with as it was. All of the world's wrongdoings had fallen onto that plate, and I could only imagine how busy Karma could be while at work. Seeing as I carried out my own work, however, what I realized was that it was an arduous yet fun job to carry out. In some ways, I envied Karma for all that it got to do to people. Any anger I had within me could be taken out on people, and it would be for all of the right reasons!

The form of comeuppance I had chosen was to poison others. I could not have them ruining my chances with Karma or my reputation. If they got to talk to everyone else, then I would have no chance at achieving what I wanted. I couldn't have everyone on my side if I let them off the hook too easily. Furthermore, I couldn't have this found out about me; if I had been outed like that, then nobody would take my side and Karma would not notice anything I had done to make the load lighter.

A girl I knew in high school had decided to cut class with me. Unfortunately, we had been caught, and my dad was furious about the ordeal. But the tension was too much for me to bear; it was her fault that we even ditched in the first place, anyway. So I put poison in her drink while she was not looking. That ought to keep her from talking, especially when I told my dad that it was her fault that we ditched. He didn't have to know that I was the reason she stopped coming around; he forbade me from associating with her after that, anyhow. It had all worked out for the better.

A different girl I knew had been my friend for a while. Over the years, however, we began to drift apart. She joked around too much, even when it was supposed to be serious. On top of that, she was putting on weight. We ate the same thing at lunch every day, but outside of school, I ate so much better than she did. I even told her this! But nobody could know that I cared this much about appearances; I had to be the positive one in every way possible. Every little thing involving some sort of justice or positivity, I had to be part of, or else they would know so much more easily and I would not be able to achieve my goals. Therefore, she had to go, before she could tell other people. She knew too much about me, and it would only get in my way. That, and she had higher grades than I did. What if she looked smarter than me?

One day, she had asked me to help her in getting a ride to a meetup. I initially agreed, and I had left some poison in her water bottle while having visited her one day. When she had asked me once more when my other friends and I were coming to get her, she had already drunk her poison. I could tell; her messages and her phone calls became all the more frantic. Before it could all take effect at once, I finally told her the truth; we were never going to bring her along with us.

In the meantime, I began to date a guy. I had to admit, this was some of my best work yet. My aforementioned friend who needed a ride had mentioned to me that he used her and abused her. It couldn't be that simple; surely he had to have a side to his story. Either way, I wanted him, and I couldn't help the feelings that I had for him, just because she didn't get what she wanted from him. I convinced him to add more poison to her drink while she wasn't looking when we saw her while we were out and about together. When she made eye contact with me, I assured her of one thing I was certain of.

"He'll change for me."

Now that she was out of the picture, though, I had him to myself. Besides, he would totally change for me. I did not need the likes of her breathing down my neck about it and reminding me of what she told me, much less going and telling everyone about it.

Unfortunately, that relationship ended up failing. No matter; I was still justified in all of my decisions up to this point. But seeing as I was able to secure a different relationship so quickly, and with his best friend no less, the problem did not lie with me. It lied with the people who had to be cut off; it was never me.

Then this other girl I knew just had to say something about the things I posted on my public profiles. She should not have been able to see them! Who was she to say that I was an arrogant bully or to criticize me? Everyone whom I talked about online had it coming, and she was nobody. I used social media as an outlet to vent. Here I was holding people accountable for having irresponsibly posted months prior, and she was stalking a post I made a few days ago. I was trying to be nice to her, but now she had to go. She should have just known that I was done with her and no longer needed her.

She wanted to die, even after she attempted to make things right. At this rate, she brought it upon herself and drank the poison while I had barely lifted a finger to do anything. It was all her fault, anyway. Always, she had excelled at everything I could not handle. She spoke

Spanish, a language that was in *my* heritage, not hers, and she pursued honors, and it made me look bad when I was too busy to constantly stay in contact with everyone, too busy to keep up good enough grades to have the same prestige as her.

After all of that, large crowds of people decided that I was wrong about everything. About holding people accountable, about the things I was saying, and about speaking "over" entire groups of people I did not belong to. I was speaking for them, and for the record, they should be grateful for all that I had done for them. Even after I shared what my own background was, those ingrates only made fun of me for speaking out for others, told me that I just made everything about myself. They were telling me that it did not offend them and that I did not speak for everyone, but they clearly did not know how it was affecting them. A makeup style was everything, and the makeup style I had pointed out to everybody clearly mocked how different ethnic groups looked while those fools ate it up. How could a group of people who try to make themselves look Asian have a bigger following than me? I was a good person, and I stood for the right thing. I was unique.

Everyone just wanted to hate me for no reason at this point. Even my own parents were so self absorbed and narcissistic. I had contemplated slowly poisoning them over time, but there was too much for me to consider, in spite of the trauma they put me through. They had been divorced, and I claimed my mother's heritage while being raised primarily by my father. In reality, I could not stand either of them. Despite my pride in my mother's heritage, she was an irresponsible drunk who only cared about herself and her party music. And despite my father's responsibility in raising me, he was at fault for being too strict to me. He was so rigid in his conservative beliefs, and he never admitted when he was wrong.

There was yet another friend of mine I was done with. The issue was that we had gossiped plenty together, so she had all of the dirt on me. We even gossiped about the other girls I mentioned before. But if she was to ruin me, then I could not allow that. I was sure that for now I was safe, but one could never be too sure for too long. While the fact that she was overweight made me the prettier friend by default, it was still a pain to be seen with her. She relied on her ringlets to frame her face in order to keep her from resembling the Michelin Man, and while it boosted my ego, I knew she was planning to get rid of me. I had to get rid of her first.

I planned to meet with her for dinner one night, and I awaited her at a table to come join me. I always carried the poison on me, just in case I needed it. It felt like a good idea to at least start to get her out of the picture. A waitress passed me by, and she set the two menus down before me while I waited for my friend to join me. My hands folded in front of me, and I began to twiddle my thumbs while waiting. My eyes darted to the waitress, who was serving food to everyone else. Clearly, I was the healthiest one in the room, considering that I ordered the healthiest thing on the menu.

"Excuse me?" I asked, stopping the waitress as she set down my water. "Have you seen a curly haired brunette come in yet?"

"No, she isn't here yet." She answered me.

The waitress walked away from me while I patiently waited for my friend to come join me. My patience was rapidly thinning. I sipped my water, tapping my fingers against the counter.

"Excuse me." I called out again, being ignored. "Excuse me!"

"Ma'am, there are other customers I must tend to. What is it?" The waitress had the nerve to sound exasperated. No matter; I could act patiently for a little longer.

"I just have to meet with my friend. Are you sure she hasn't slipped in at all?" I asked.

"Nobody like the person you described has come in." She answered, walking away from me and earning an irritated huff from me in response.

At this point, I received a text message. My friend's sister got a hold of me, apologizing for the fact that she would not be able to make it.

This caught me by surprise; someone surely must have gotten to her before I could. The notion heavily irritated me, even if it meant that I could not be blamed for any of it. As I looked over the text to confirm for myself, I huffed and slammed my hand down onto the table.

"Karma's a bitch!" I exclaimed, not even paying mind to the shocked faces around me. They were nobodies, and my outburst would be yesterday's news in no time.

I figured I would save the poison for another time. I would need it one day, would I not? Who was to say that nobody else would threaten to turn on me? Like my quieter friend, but I doubt she would ever raise her voice enough to actually say anything or to criticize me. Or a male friend of mine who was not man enough to ever say anything negative about me. So long as they stayed on my side, I had to be just fine. But I still had my ways should they or anyone try to turn their back on me when I was trying to be nice about it.

I heard rumors of a lady who wished to help others with achieving their vengeance. If you helped her, then she would help you. I was unsure as to how she might do that, but I more than welcomed anyone wanting to help me get what I wanted. I fully intended to find her, because I did not want to be uselessly doing things for other people forever. However, it would build upon my reputation, and it would make the useless people want to say good things about me. So I supposed this was not for naught; I could sooner be in good graces with much more significant people, and no longer need the lowly losers my life left me with.

One day, I received an invitation to an older woman's house. I had not been asked to do anything for her; she simply wanted company. Lonely old people had plenty of nice things to be offered, and they could be quite hospitable when they wanted to. Not a complete waste of time, I supposed. The house was not too far from where I lived, though my dad and I lived in an apartment. This lady had to have played her cards right, to be able to own a house. It was unfortunate, my dad not knowing how to play the game right and leaving me with a home that had to be paid into forever and ever, a home that had to be *rented.* I prepared my things before going over to this old lady's place, noticing that my dad was watching TV. He had so many things to work through, and he was sitting there like he was comfortable with himself?

"I'm going out." I told him, only for him to look my way.

"Don't get yourself into too much trouble," he told me. "Where are you going?"

"This old lady's place. Seems kinda lonely." I shrugged.

"Have fun," he added with a nonchalant wave of a hand while looking for something else to watch. How could he change it from the news and miss out on the injustices plaguing us? He could at least be more aware of them, instead of turning it to some distraction or some alternative news source that would make him more ignorant than he already was.

I was relieved that he wasn't bothering me about my employment anymore. He would never consider what I did previously as actual work, but it involved real work. There were people who wanted to buy pictures of me with little to no clothing. I was practically doing anyone who wanted them a huge favor by doing this. However, it never took off into the career I wanted, and I only looked like I was doing nothing, which upset my father. I just couldn't deal with retail anymore.

Upon arriving at the old woman's house, I knocked on the door, waiting and wondering if I would need to let myself in. I mean, who knew if she would be too slow to do so or if she died and needed me to go and tell everybody? If it weren't for me, nobody would know anything happened to her, seeing as she seemed quite reclusive and like she minded her business for the most part. Nobody seemed to pay her much mind, and I hardly saw anyone come to see this house. The door opened, and it revealed a sweet looking woman who was ready to greet me with a smile.

"I hope I haven't kept you waiting for too long." Her voice proved elegant and sophisticated, the kind of person I could see myself being around already. While she was old, she took care to keep herself presentable. "Please, come in. I've just made tea."

I entered the woman's home, looking around me and taking in the decor. Red silk curtains hung over the windows, and the sofas were classic white, not the modern kind that broke easily. The ostentatious nature of it made me wonder just what she did for a living, what sort of life she led. That, or the sort of support she had and what sort of person she was, if it was others who helped her to get to this point. What a luxury it was, to have people who didn't drag her down like the people I had.

"Have a seat. I will join you shortly." She gestured toward the seating area for me, bringing out the teapot. Already, the cups and silverware had been set up for us to enjoy our time together. Fine china of this quality was not expected. It was about time I was treated to something that I deserved.

"You have a lovely place." I could not get over how wonderful her place looked. Sure, there were things I would have done differently had it been my own, but she had exquisite taste, her home well maintained as if to be proudly showcased to guests. In speaking of taste, the snacks she had to provide looked decadent and expertly prepared; with her sophisticated nature, it wouldn't surprise me either way if she could prepare them with such skill herself or if she bought them from a high-end baker.

"I do take pride in what is mine and try to take care of it." The elder replied, taking her seat across from me and observing me with patience and gesturing toward the pastries. "Do help yourself."

I noticed she had some tea in her cup already, and with a smile, she took the scalding pot of tea by its handle and poured me a cup. An array of additives sat before us, and I contemplated trying it with and without sugar. Anything that I did felt lesser than in her presence somehow, yet she never made me self conscious about it. If anything, her presence had reassured me that I was doing nothing wrong; all I was was a guest in her home enjoying what she had to offer.

"A bit bitter, I take it?" She inquired with the slightest tilt of her head.

"No, no! It's wonderful." I assured her.

"If you have a taste for the sweeter things, that's what I brought the sugar and cream out for. Look, you even have yourself some honey."

I decided to take her up on the offer to sweeten it up a little, adding a splash of milk to the tea and some honey. I mixed it in, taking a piece of lemon cake provided on the delicate, fancy platter she brought forward. Her hands folded in front of her as she watched me, and I covered my mouth as I mulled over what I would ask her. I was growing more and more curious by the minute, especially as to who she was and why she chose to invite me of all people.

"I am so sorry I never asked," I said once I swallowed my cake. "What is your name? I don't think I have seen much of you around here."

"Oh, this is a fun little game I like to play." She responded with a giggle. "Let's see if you can guess what it is before our little visit is over."

My brow raised at her suggestion. Although it was a strange idea, I liked it! The idea of playing a game to guess was quite fun, even if unheard of.

"Let's see… Ethel, Elizabeth, Anne, Florence?" I attempted to guess, using a healthy mixture of typical old lady names and ones that I found sophisticated. It would fit her nature to have a classy name.

"I'll give you a hint, and clear some boring guesses off the table." She told me. "Try to think… Not a typical name. Yes, I am certainly one of a kind."

"Wow, just like me!" I exclaimed excitedly. "I might need another hint here… Aster, Amaryllis, Celestina…"

"Not quite." She shook her head, confirming that all of my guesses were incorrect. "Think more… Abstract. Most would not think to associate my name with me. Oh, and here's a bonus hint; my name does not start with any letter that the previous names began with."

"Abstract... Honor, Love..." I guessed, sipping more of my tea and deciding I would add some sugar to it.

"Nice guesses, but no." She shook her head calmly, her voice continuing to lull and to maintain a calming effect. "If anything, most would say that I am cold, and others say I am sweet. In that case, I would have guessed that I'm ice cream."

"Revenge is a silly name!" I laughed, drinking up more of my tea.

In response, she only smiled and watched me drink, then standing up. "Not quite, but you are rather close. Do enjoy yourself, have a bite of some more cake. The tea washes it down exquisitely, don't you think?"

"It does. In fact, I think I'd like some more." I requested politely, holding the cup for her before she poured more into my cup.

As I added my sugar in, I began to feel unsettled. The world around me did not seem as it previously was; it spun too fast. Fear began to fill me to the brim. But it couldn't be her, right? She was so hospitable, and she looked wise enough not to poison my food. Then again, I couldn't account for her old age. No, I was being ridiculous.

"Oh, dear, you look like you've seen a ghost. Take another sip of your tea." She suggested with concern, watching me patiently as I took another sip. "Have you any other guesses as to who I am? You may know more than you currently think. But you're about to realize that you know nothing about me."

I drank more, figuring I would not add any more flavoring to it. Perhaps this was the way it ought to be enjoyed, and I was not accustomed to the sort of luxuries she clearly had at her disposal. I hoped that it would wash whatever was bugging me down my throat.

"In the meantime, you can think back to all of the people you have wronged."

I began to cough, though I couldn't tell whether it was my coughing or her words that made me fall out of my chair and onto the floor. My eyes widened as I faced her, wondering just why I was feeling this way. What had I done to deserve this?

"I have heard of the things you seek." The old woman began to step closer to me, looking down at me as I curled up on the floor and coughed more, sweat drenching my skin as my heart raced. "You wish to hold others accountable, yet you cannot do the same for yourself. What good would you be to hold others accountable, when you cannot confront your own injustices? When you assert yourself as an authority when you truly have none to claim?"

I couldn't even defend myself. Any excuse I could come up with was actively being replaced by my own choking and coughing. The old woman approached me, grasping me by the chin and forcing me to face her.

"Karma's a bitch, you say?" She questioned with a raised brow. "Oh, no, honey. Karma is a classy, wise elder that will calmly sit you down and serve you tea you later realize was laced with the same poison you served others for years."

I had to force myself to sputter out what I wanted to say. Or, at least, part of it. "Y-You…"

Her brows raised as she awaited the rest of my sentence. Seeing as I couldn't finish it, she took it upon herself to do so for me.

"I am Karma," she explained. "The one others seek out, offering help to. After what I saw you put your friends through, I decided I could not sit back and allow it. And you had the gall to come looking for me to seek a favor? That is just rich. As if I can't see through people like you. To think of how kind your friends were to you… But let me guess. You think that you're too good for them, and for you to be in their presence graces them. I imagine that this has to do with how unique you think you are. Just so we're clear, unique does not mean useful."

As I kept struggling to breathe, I saw those old friends once more. The ones I poisoned, anyhow. All three of them looked down at me while I struggled, contemptuous sneers formed on their faces. A sight I would never forget, as I was confronted with their suffering and triumph over me.

The World is Ours

"Pure turmoil" were the only words able to describe the horrific scene of the earth. Structures of any kind—residual, decorative, living—were obliterated and collapsed to the ground. Individuals who wished to do good to the world, were now unable, because they, as well as the place they wished to change, were destroyed.

Automobiles were flipped over, crushed in the most brutal ways possible. People appeared slain by the catastrophe, hardly any of the faces appearing to have gone calmly. Buildings were on their sides, with their tops ripped off violently and their glass shattered.

In all of this chaos, there was a young girl sitting on the ground. Now she would not have people to care for her, people to learn from, people to teach, or people to love. She sat with a blank expression in all of the chaos. She had shed, or believed she had shed, any tears left within her. She looked around, wondering if such an atrocious sight of the world was real.

"I cannot be the only one here," she thought.

In another half of the world was a young boy, sitting in similar turmoil. He, too, had lost everything that truly mattered. He lost two strict yet loving people, people who had ever thought dearly of him. He checked his surroundings as well, wondering if all had truly gone from the world he knew.

"There is no way I can be alone," he said to himself.

The girl had an idea. She decided she would search for companionship. She stood up. Silence filled the atmosphere across the entire earth.

"Hello," she called. "Is there anyone else out there? Hello?"

Her call rang out around the earth. The boy heard it and could not believe he heard a voice. Hope was not lost yet.

"Hello," the boy called. "Who's out there?"

The girl heard his voice. She wondered if this could be real. After a few seconds of being struck with awe, she finally responded.

"I want a friend," she shouted. "We can find each other and not be lonely."

"I want to find you," the boy said. "I will be your friend."

"I'll come for you," they said simultaneously, not realizing that they both said it.

They both began to walk. They began the search for companionship. Life can't be lived alone. They passed people who were gone for eternity. How long is eternity?

The girl knelt by people she passed and left a kiss on their foreheads. She was growing tired, but remained relentless at finding this new friend. She was resourceful and built a raft to use on water. She wore a hood that one of the bodies wore, figuring that they would not need it anymore. The hood would provide warmth in times of cold. She scoured the areas she passed for food.

The boy sat by people he passed and said a prayer for them. He was exhausted but would not stop at his search for a companion. He took no breaks. He used items that would not be used by the countless corpses he passed. He was careful to not eat too much, as the person he searched for may need it.

They had circled around the planet looking for each other. The girl realized this due to how she saw the faces of those she knew in her area once again. She fell to her knees and mourned them. The boy recognized the area itself, sadly reminiscing of his fond memories with a refined bitterness. They both wondered if the faces they had seen and knew were real or illusions. Was loneliness in the world reality? Were the people we knew simply illusionary?

They both began to think that the voice of the other was merely a part of their imagination. Despite this, they kept moving towards each other. The years that passed them as they had passed the same dead people were somber and tiring.

Now that the boy began taking breaks more than usual, the girl was starting to catch up to him. The girl stayed relentless in her search for a friend. One day, the boy, who had skipped breakfast and lunch to spend more time looking for a fellow survivor, was too tired to stay up any longer. He had collapsed after praying for a couple of dead people.

The girl arrived at the area where the boy was lying. She knelt by the bodies to kiss them on their foreheads. One of those bodies was the body of the boy. When she kissed the forehead of the boy, she felt something she had not in a while; warmth. She was startled. She realized that this person was alive. She brought him to a less cluttered area and gave him her hooded cloak as a blanket.

When the boy woke up, he saw the girl hovering over him.

"Oh good, you're awake," she smiled.

The boy reached his hand out to touch the girl's face. This girl was no illusion.

She was as real as he was.

"Are you..." He asked. "Her?"

He could not think of anything else to call her. He only remembered the voice he heard being feminine.

The girl was taken aback. She realized that she had arrived at the voice she heard several years ago.

"You're the boy who answered me," she said.

They realized that they were not alone. They could live the horrors of reality together.

"How long I've been looking for you!" The girl said.

"I was beginning to think that the people around me were fake," the boy said.

"Me too."

"We can talk about what our lives used to be. We can decide the fate of humanity. There is nothing we can't do."

"We have no limits. We can do whatever we want."

"The world is ours," they said simultaneously.

They lived together and moved together. They agreed to look for any more living people who could join them. They were no longer lonely.

Reunited

The day I came into the world, I was not yet ready. There was no time to understand what was happening to me or why I needed to come out so soon. Already, I was here, regardless of how unprepared I was for this. Nobody could have expected me to be ready.

Once I was out, I was handed over to my mama. I knew she was my mama, because I could smell her and feel her. Everything about her felt familiar and comforting, even if I was on the outside now. I struggled, but everyone around me tried to make me comfortable. The lights were bright, so bright that it hurt my eyes, but I was kept warm by my mama. As warm as I could be, at least; it was so much warmer on the inside. But here I was, in my mama's arms. It was the best place I could be in, even as I fought to breathe. Being on the outside was not easy for me so far; there was a tube pushed into my mouth, and there were many things attached to me. They were all sticky. I did not know why, but they stuck them all over my body. My mama also had things stuck to her. Was this what being on the outside meant?

I had looked forward to this day, getting to meet my mama. Her hair was colored pink, yet it was the only bright thing that did not hurt my eyes. Nothing about my mama would hurt my eyes; I enjoyed every second I got to see her. From inside out, I felt her love for me. She was a being filled with warmth and love alike. The look in her hazel eyes was tired, yet hopeful, as if to say she counted on me. She believed in me, and she was so happy to see me. The hope in her eyes made it worthwhile to have come out earlier than expected. I would do all that I could to make her happy. I was her strong, handsome boy. I know this, because she told me so.

It grew harder and harder for me to breathe. I tried and tried as much as I could; I didn't want my mama to stop being happy. Worry grew in her, yet she held me all the same. She was my source of comfort and warmth. While she held me, the people around us gifted us with nice things for me, and they stood in front of us while they held devices which made shuttering noises. Blankets, clothes made to my proportions, and a little heart shaped pillow. At one point, they took my hand and my feet and pressed them against a pad of some sort. Somehow, it made pictures of my hand and my feet when they pressed them against pieces of paper. They were tiny, compared to everyone else. I was tiny. I felt strength with the warmth and the love as my mama held me. She spoke to me, her voice gentle and full of love. It was hard to breathe, but I would keep trying for her. My mama did everything she could for me; I had to try for her, even if it hurt. She fought for me, so I had to fight for her.

However, it was harder and harder for me to fight. I tried my best, I really did, Mama. I wanted to spend more time and to be with my mama. But I was too sensitive to everything. I was not ready for this world, not yet. But I didn't want to go, either. I had barely gotten to hear my mama tell me my name, to hear her tell me that she loved me as she held me on the outside. All of it was happening too fast for my liking. There was unrest, and I could tell it was all because of me. Everyone tried so hard for me. I was sorry that I wasn't able to, because they all tried to keep me here.

As comfortable as I became, it became all the more appealing for me to rest. I just hoped everyone would give my mama love and dote on her like she doted on me. And I hoped that she knew that I was sorry and that I loved her with all of my being. To see that her hope amounted to this broke my heart, but I wanted her to know that I would be okay. She did everything she could for me.

As my eyes closed, I stopped moving. Nothingness. I was no longer in pain, and it wasn't hard to breathe anymore.

But then, there was a bright light. Only this time, the bright light didn't hurt. I was warm again. It was as if my mama handed me over to someone else; I was in someone else's arms now. These arms were warm and comfortable like my mama's, yet they were more experienced. I could tell that this person had a lot of experience with holding babies.

"Well, hiya, darlin'." She greeted me when I looked up at her. Her hair was curly, and the curls looked poofy and gray. This lady's eyes were blue.

I looked all around me, able to understand yet struggling to grasp everything. It all happened too fast; I had no chance to make any sense of what happened. One thing I did understand was that I felt whole, like nothing was rushed while I was being created. There was no more pain, no more need to fight.

"Who are you?" I asked aloud. I was able to speak.

"I am the mother of the father of the father of your mother." The lady explained. "I am your great great grandma. It's nice to meet you. When I saw you, I knew you were mine, you know. We have a damn good lookin' family."

My mama had handed me over to my great great grandma. Everything around us was different from where I was with my mama; did we go somewhere else while I rested? Everything surrounding us looked soft and white. My great great grandma walked past a gate, and still everything ahead of us looked so soft and inviting. I looked around for her, wanting to ensure that my mama was with us. Where did she go?

"Where is Mama?" I asked her.

"She's still recovering," my great great grandma said, "Having a baby is tough on a mama's body. Not to mention losing a baby."

"Losing? But I'm right here." I retorted with a frown.

My smiling grandmother suddenly grew grim. There was a truth she wished she could hide from me, and hide me from. However, there came a point that I needed to know.

"I'm sorry, darlin'." She told me. "Some little ones don't make it. You were sent here a little early. Even if I'm glad to have one of you with me, I wish it could have been later down the line."

I remembered, then, how hard it was for me to breathe. How hard it was to hold on, even when I willed myself to for my mama. There were so many things that I didn't get to do, and so many people I was supposed to meet. All I did was rest, yet that was when I was handed over to my great great grandma. That moment was when I left my tiny body behind, I realized as I rewatched the scene. That, alongside leaving a hole in my mama's heart.

It made my heart ache unbelievably to see her grieve; didn't she know I was okay now? I wished I could tell her myself. I could even speak now. I watched as she clung onto the things that belonged to me, as if trying to keep any piece of me alive that she could. She was welcome to keep all of those things; if it made her even a little happy, then that was what I wanted. Tears filled her eyes, and I wanted nothing more than to make them stop. My mama felt like nothing would ever be good again, not without me in the world. All I could do was watch. I wished she could hear me. “Don’t cry, Mama.” I wanted to reach out and touch her, to grab onto her finger; it made her so happy when I did that, even with my limited strength.

“Believe me, kiddo, I’ve tried.” My grandmother told me. “They hardly ever hear us or see us.”

To prove it to me, my grandmother allowed me to see the pain a lot of other people were in when she had passed away. She, too, wished desperately that she could convince them all to stop crying. Additionally, she gave me the chance to realize that all of them were *my* family, too. There were so many lovely faces that I never got to meet; I came and went too quickly for any of them to have a chance. My grandma was right; our family, in spite of how different they looked from each other, were all beautiful. Good looking, as she put it; I thought that if I got to look at them while staying with mama, that they wouldn’t have hurt my eyes either.

“You may have gone early, but at least you weren’t put through more pain than you had to be.” She tried to encourage me to look on the bright side. At that moment, I began to watch her lived experiences. Heartbreak, she learned about firsthand, and she felt it in more ways than I had. Not to mention the pain inflicting her as people around her had passed away; all I could think of was how my mama watched me pass away, and my great great grandma had seen it with young people and old people alike. It never hurt any less, no matter the loss; my grandma lost a child who got to be a grandma herself, and it still left a hole in her heart. There was plenty of pain that she had been put through over the course of her life, yet there were also treasured moments that she and those around her got to cherish. She had her own babies, and then those babies grew up and had their own babies, and then those babies grew up and had their own babies, and then some of those babies grew up and had their own babies. My great great grandma had a big family, and she did a lot for them. She lived, and she had gotten the chance to do things for others.

"You touched so many people." I told her. "I wish I could have touched more people."

"I wouldn't say you didn't." My grandmother replied. "Take a look and see for yourself."

At that moment, I was shown different people. All of these people were meant to be my family, and yet I did not get to meet any of them. They were washed over with sadness and heartbreak, unable to believe that I had been stolen from this world so soon. Some cried, some couldn't face their sadness and turned to other emotions, such as anger or recklessness. But the root cause was all the same; all of them were sad.

In particular, there was a lady who caught my attention. Her hair was golden, and her eyes were blue. She closed the door, taking notice of a stuffed toy in her room that she bought and meant to give to me. As she held the toy, she crumpled to the floor and cried ceaselessly. Her mind had been filled with images of herself getting to hold me and to dote on me, all for it to be taken away from her. *It's not fair. He should've gotten to live and be loved.* She thought to herself. Prior to this, she saw photos of me that my mama had shared on a place called the Internet. In particular, a place called Facebook.

Her hands folded together, and her head bowed with her eyes closed. She was asking someone named God to take me into His arms, and for Him to comfort my mama. I liked her for that. This is a cousin. This is one of many cousins.

I saw her past; when she and my mama were bigger babies, they took off everywhere they could together as soon as they saw each other. Their lives were intertwined, there was no doubt about that. As babies, as children, as teenagers, as adults, they always ran off together. Nobody could keep up with them; they were in their own world.

And now here everyone was, feeling sad. Other family members heard my tale, and it brought them grief too. I did not want this; the whole world was in tears because of me. I looked up at my grandma.

"I don't want to touch people like this." I said. "They're all sad. Did I give everyone pain?"

"Not necessarily." My grandma said. "Take another look."

The same lady I saw was then inspired; she wanted to write a story about me. I watched as she fought through tears to create something good out of tragedy. I could tell that she hoped my mama would like it. She was determined; she had to write it as best as she could, and to make me known despite what little time I had spent being alive.

And then there was my mama; she was doing everything with me on her mind. As painful as it was for her to lose me, she thinks of what could make me proud. She knows I'm watching her from above, and she knows that I am proud of her. I could not have picked someone better to be my mama, even with the short time I had with her. I was grateful for each and every second I spent in her arms, and she appeared to be honored that she held me for the entirety of my life. I hope she was; I always wanted her to be proud of me.

Knowing this gave me peace. As long as she knew that she did the best she could, and that I was okay now, I was happy. Many other smiling faces, who had been here with my grandma, surrounded us, wanting to greet me. Many of them, too, were family, and all of them wanted to see me.

I am warm. I am loved. I am remembered.

"By the way, Grandma, what's your name?" I asked, seeing as I had all of eternity to learn about her and our family.

In Loving Memory

Kyro (September 27, 2021 - September 27, 2021)

Grandma Betty (September 1, 1931 - December 7, 2019)

The Lake Nymph

Nevaeh was a bubbly, social girl who seemed to always have a smile on her face. She was beautiful, intelligent, and sweet. Her family and friends marveled at everything she did because she did it flawlessly, for her perfectionism would not allow a mistake. This, of course, was simply her way of trying to make others happy. As a result, her academic success decorated her, and she wore this success proudly.

What lied beneath the surface, however, was lack of satisfaction and emptiness. She did not regard herself as any of the things many praised her for, and she concerned herself with these perceived flaws, namely with the way that she had not explored much outside of school. As much as extracurriculars could expose her to different experiences, most of these were under the control of her school, thus, in her mind, not allowing the full experience of freedom. She had not connected with nature, yet she learned of the different biological and chemical compounds which made it up. She studied arduously for her tests to achieve top scores, yet this dedicated time studying kept her from going out. Even if she went to the mall with friends, which she rarely did due to her studies, she still was in a heavily controlled environment. The limited interaction left her drained; she needed more connection, yet she was thrust back into her duties as a student. Her strict approach to her studies, of course, was self imposed, yet she insisted upon it nonetheless.

A rebellious sense came over her one day, as if she had no control of it. This rebellion, however, was only against herself and the strict rules she put in place for herself; her parents took no issue with her going out, as they would sooner assume she was kidnapped or somehow held up than think she would deliberately run off elsewhere that deviated from her normal routine. Something compelled her to go out, or so she convinced herself. Then again, it was difficult to distinguish whether something called out to her, or if her own desire for connection drove her so crazy that she sought out some sort of thrill, something different from her ordinary life. She swore she told herself to stay in her room and to bury herself in calculus. However, the thought of having to do so was maddening, so much so that she needed escape. Then again, her parents were not the overly strict type to desperately need escaping from; that label was reserved specifically for Nevaeh herself, seeing as she imposed her own regulations on herself to operate as a top student. Despite this, she never regarded herself as better than anyone else, nor did she see her classmates as competition. The competition was herself, and her challenge was to outdo herself each and every day. Said competition with herself, however, was tiring.

Nevaeh neared the lake, staring curiously into the water. She could not for the life of her figure out why she came out here, even after she told herself she would stay in her room and study for the test the next day. She could have chosen a better day, with the skies so full of clouds and gray. Nonetheless, here she was, staring out into the water. In spite of how cold it was outside, the water itself invited her to jump in. She hesitated, yet the idea was incredibly tempting to her. As she mulled over whether or not to jump in and whether she would swim in her clothes or run home for a bathing suit, a mysterious entity came out of the water, staring curiously at her. Nevaeh jumped as she watched said entity, initially believing that she was another person who came to swim in the lake. Then again, there was nobody else; could there have been a reason why hardly anyone else was present? Even with the wind, this lake had quite the view, and nobody should miss the chance to see. It was surrounded by lush greenery, not a dead plant in sight. The rocks led into the depths of the water, which were mysterious enough yet instilled curiosity into the mind the way Nevaeh instilled self discipline. Before she had time to process anything, she was already rattling off nervously.

"Sorry, I didn't know the lake was occupied…" Nevaeh smiled, seeming all the more uncertain of herself than her normal smiley self would have led anyone to believe. "I could leave, if you'd prefer that. I just… I don't know what came over me."

The entity stared at her, which only added to her nervousness. It made her feel as if *she* were the abnormal one, the non-human, yet this entity bore no judgment for her. In fact, she reached forward, gently cupping Nevaeh's face as if to get a better look at her. Nevaeh found herself wanting to question what the entity was doing, yet she fell silent, as if she were commanded to.

"... Stay." The entity spoke, seeming perfectly unbothered by the chilly weather.

"... What are you, exactly?" Nevaeh finally mustered up the words she wished to use. She eyed the bottom of the entity's dress, which hid the lower half of her body. "Are you… A mermaid?"

The entity only smiled at her. "No. A nymph."

"Oh! My apologies." Nevaeh seemed embarrassed to have mistaken her for the wrong supernatural creature. It only created more questions in her mind as to what was happening, and if there were other mythological creatures out there, if the one before her knew any of them. That seemed so preposterous, to assume that this nymph would know other mysterious entities.

Before she knew it, the nymph was pulling her toward the water. Somehow, Nevaeh felt she could trust her, that she would keep her safe. Any concern was quickly replaced with confusion; the nymph pressed her lips against hers. However, Nevaeh soon found that this was only so she could breathe beneath the water; the nymph pulled her under suddenly, and Nevaeh realized that she did not have to hold her breath. The nymph found amusement in Nevaeh's initial attempt to hold her breath, as well as the realization that struck her newfound human friend.

Nevaeh looked over the nymph, wondering what she wanted her in the water for. However, she realized she was still in her clothes; that would be troublesome when she got home later. Her parents were sure to be puzzled by the fact that her clothes were soaked with lake water. Surprisingly enough, she was not weighed down by her clothes. Perhaps it was a good thing she forgot her jacket. The nymph especially felt no such constraint herself, as if her clothes were designed for the water. Her feet stuck out from under the long skirt, thus confirming that her legs were legs and not one joint limb, like Nevaeh would have expected a mermaid to have. But the nymph, like a mermaid, was fully capable of breathing underwater. Furthermore, she gave a human that same ability. Nevaeh could only rationalize this by thinking of CPR, though that was used to save someone from the brink of death, someone who *almost* drowned. In this case, however, it was to prevent her from drowning, to allow her to play beneath the surface without the need to go back up for air.

The lake hid many wonders, which caused Nevaeh to wonder how nobody else discovered such beauty before. Had this nymph been waiting to meet someone? It only made Nevaeh ponder how lonely the poor thing was for so long. Perhaps it was a good thing Nevaeh made the time to come out and to happen upon this lake for herself. With all of its undiscovered beauty, the lake introduced a privilege to her that appeared to not have been introduced to any other human. Only the fish in this lake, and perhaps fellow nymphs that this one knew (which she hoped; loneliness was maddening). There were all sorts of organisms Nevaeh learned about in class that had to be in this water, yet she was not here to conduct scientific research or to take notes. All she was required to do was to appreciate the things that she continuously got to see without having to stop to go back up. She allowed the nymph to guide her, swimming deeper and deeper all while marveling at the fact that she was still alive with no need to resurface. And still, there was light. Of course, the notion of descending into the darkness crept into her mind, yet the nymph was entirely unfazed. Nevaeh hoped that with her ability to breathe underwater that she would also be able to see underwater. Her optimism and her evidence to trust the nymph so far allowed her to feel safe; surely no harm would come her way.

As the two of them neared the bottom of the lake, there were lights which paved the way. This offered relief to Nevaeh, who was grateful to be able to see these things so much more clearly. An underwater city, which she wondered was abandoned or if it was even discovered. Were these the ruins, or was it only the beginning? Had it been the beginning, it surely would have been difficult for the nymph to accomplish all on her own. The process of establishing an underwater city, one which most would not have the chance to admire, had to be a tiring one. One which most would not see the efforts for, and ultimately…

A thankless task.

"Come," the nymph gestured for the girl to follow her, "look at the things I've made."

The structures within the lake were carved. There was no perfectionistic edge to them, yet this made them different and all the more beautiful for it. If Nevaeh had to wager a guess, she would have guessed these were salt rocks. However, the implication that the nymph was the one behind this further impressed her. The artistic structure of these rock formations would have surely earned her an A in her art class, or perhaps ceramics. Wait, what was she doing, thinking about school at a time like this? Thoughts of her grades were all too embedded into her mind; she came out here to unwind, yet she could not get any of it off her mind. The deep greens in the lake complemented the deep blues, and these colors contrasted the brighter green of the grass surrounding the lake as well as the plants at the surface of the water, the plants which had warmly welcomed Nevaeh into the lake along the simple brown sand. The invitation into this lake, onto this adventure with this nymph of the lake, must have been what compelled her to go out in the first place as opposed to her preplanned study session, so she figured.

"This is impressive…" Nevaeh remarked, drinking in her surroundings. The natural beauty of it all could readily intoxicate her, and it would be an intoxication that she would be more than happy to seek out again. "Why in the bottom of the lake?"

"It is my home." The nymph answered simply. "I do what I like with my home."

"My bad." Nevaeh said, causing the nymph to giggle.

"Why do you apologize?" She tilted her head. "And so often, too."

"Right, my mistake." Nevaeh said.

"There has been no mistake." The nymph said. "There has been no bad. You are a learner."

"I certainly like to think of myself as one." Nevaeh said bashfully.

"A quick learner, too." The nymph added. "It would be nice to have someone here… But you, you have your own home."

At this moment, Nevaeh began to think of her family; surely she would need to go back to them at some point. It would be immensely cruel to make her parents worry about her whereabouts, only to be unable to discover her while she swam comfortably in the bottom of a lake. Her friends at school and her teachers would be stricken with anxiety at the thought of her disappearing, never to be heard from again. As morbid as it was, she also took her grades into consideration; they would fall should she not stay on top of them. However, something told her that this was not as important. A significant weight had been lifted off of her chest, allowing her to feel as if she could breathe. She thought such relief was only attainable through her summer breaks, or through finally getting through school and being done. Even if temporarily, she rid herself of academic stress and thoughts of everyday life.

"I don't want to leave yet." Nevaeh told the nymph. "I know I'll have to, but I'm not ready."

"It's hard, going back to things you don't want to do." The nymph told her. "But you are a human, and that is what humans are designed for."

"Yes, thank you for the reminder." Nevaeh replied sarcastically.

"Haha, you humans are always so funny," the nymph laughed, creating another rock formation. Perhaps this one was a commemoration of something. But would that not mean that the other formations were significant?

Here, Nevaeh wished she brought a gift for the hospitable entity. She had been invited into her humble abode, yet she herself had nothing to offer. Nevaeh also wished she could take something with her, perhaps to prove her experience to others. Then again, that would have been rude; she offered nothing, and she did not want to steal from the nymph's home. She was raised better than to assume she could take things out of others' homes, or to ask when she provided nothing in return. It had to be offered to her first, yet she had the sneaking suspicion that nothing would be offered to her. Evidence may not have been wholly necessary though; what did she have to prove to anyone about this? Her writing assignments did not entail her discussing her experience with a supernatural entity (not that others would believe her), and her research for her science class would be impossible to conduct at the bottom of the lake. That is, without the assistance of the nymph. Who knew when she would run into a lake nymph again?

“There is something I must say about humans, though…” The nymph said pensively. “Hardly any of you come out and appreciate the art that nature offers. Your man-made art becomes so dull when your senses become dull.”

“Dull?” Nevaeh repeated incredulously, only to then think to herself that the nymph did indeed have a point.

“Dull.” The nymph reaffirmed with her eyebrows raised, the repetition piercing Nevaeh. “I really do admire man-made art, but when it’s inspired. When they create something that speaks to the soul. And for you, my hope is that you create something that speaks to people’s soul, and that it’s something you *want* to do.”

“You’ve made all this… But how many people see it?” Nevaeh asked the nymph. It felt criminal, getting to witness such beauty when others likely did not have the chance. Yet here the nymph was, creating as she saw fit regardless of who did and did not see it while simultaneously trying to encourage Nevaeh’s own creativity.

In response, the nymph only smiled. The enigmatic nature of the entity led Nevaeh to believe that only a privileged few were given the opportunity to join the nymph in the bottom of the lake. The girl pondered what the point could be if only a few could appreciate the structures the nymph constructed in her home. Nonetheless, the nymph seemed quite content to do as she pleased and to allow specific individuals to see the rock formations and the deep lake greenery. Perhaps that was what made it so special, yet Nevaeh wished this privilege was more readily available to everyone.

Nevaeh found responsibility to be quite bothersome, even when she considered the reward that it came with to bear such intense burdens and to ceaselessly study. Life was breathed into her, and it motivated and rejuvenated her. There was nothing that could stop her. As counterintuitive as it felt to throw herself right into schoolwork upon returning home, she felt vastly more confident that she could establish the necessary boundaries to take a break to go smell the roses.

"There's already so much that you *have* to do." The nymph said. "Make time for the things you enjoy, or you will live to regret it terribly."

Nevaeh watched as bubbles formed around her, and the nymph only smiled at her. Confusion overtook Nevaeh; there were so many questions that were not answered.

"Wait, I never learned your name!" She protested. "I can come back, right? When will I see you again?"

As Nevaeh desperately sought answers to her questions, she was only met with more bubbles obstructing her view of the nymph. Said bubbles also were lifting her to the surface, back to the world she belonged in. There was no time to contemplate what exactly was happening; her time was up, and it was time for her to go back above the water and to go back home.

* * *

Eventually, Nevaeh found herself lying in the sand beside the lake. She was unsure of how she got there, but she was soaking wet. The weather did not help, either; she shivered as she looked around her, then directing her gaze upward to see someone leaning over her.

"You're awake," the woman sighed in relief. "What are you doing out here, girl? Don't you suppose it's too cold to go swimming?"

"... I was sleeping?" Nevaeh asked.

"Yes, you were!" The woman said incredulously. "You must have tuckered yourself out swimming. But this isn't the best spot for a midday nap, much less without a towel or something to lay on…"

Nevaeh looked all around her, as if to search for the same mystified feeling she experienced on her little adventure with the lake nymph. It made her wonder where the nymph went, and just how long it took her to get to the surface. She never remembered losing consciousness, nor did she recall surfacing out of the water or crawling onto the sand for a nap. From this, she deduced that the nymph must have left her out to dry off and promptly disappeared after.

"Come on," the woman urged her, "let's go get you dried off. You'll catch a cold, sitting out here all damp."

"Oh, my parents are waiting for me at home." Nevaeh told the woman.

"Then they can wait a little longer for you to warm up and dry off." The woman answered her. "I know I'd be mad if my child was sent home to me soaking wet and cold… In this weather, no less! Come with me. I'll start up some soup for you."

It truly was strange for Nevaeh to have encountered such kindness on her trip out of the house. Here, she had been cautioned about strangers and their dastardly intentions, that she ought to never trust them. Surely, these warnings were not entirely without reason, considering what evils did lurk about in the world. The world around her, however, invited her and showed her hospitality. Between nature itself as well as the home of a neighboring individual she had not met before, she was nourished and cared for by the good in the world. She carried no expectations as to how she would be treated, having originally intended to take this time to be entirely by herself. There had to be some good, though, that a friend's comfort could bring. Sure, she had not known the nymph or the woman prior to her day out, yet they were friendly enough to her that she could consider them so well after this day. The comfort she did not realize that she needed, nor did she originally ask for, brought clarity to her and called into question what she really desired out of life.

Upon entering the neighbor's home, Nevaeh removed her shoes to leave them by the door and nearly sat at the table, only to be stopped by her gracious host with an abrupt "Ah, ah, ah, no! Let me get a towel before you sit down!", causing the girl to stay standing and waiting for the towel to be placed on her seat. Once the woman gestured for her to sit down before taking a larger towel and wrapping it around her shoulders. Nevaeh watched as her shoes were wrung out and hung up to dry. "Swimming in weather like this... *And* in shoes and socks. Honestly, what were you thinking, girl?"

"I don't really get the chance to do this often." Nevaeh said simply.

"You don't get the–" The woman stopped herself, shaking her head to herself. "There's better weather for this around the corner! It's a better time to go swimming then."

"I really just needed to get out of the house." Nevaeh responded. "I didn't even realize I had been so cooped up, worried about school."

The woman nodded, turning the stove on and making soup as promised. Additionally, she decided to set up some coffee. This prompted Nevaeh to look for a clock; she was unsure what time it was exactly, yet there still was light shining through the clouds as they began to dissipate. The shoes wouldn't have to be put through a dryer after all. Anyone out and about earlier that day would have easily thought that the clouds indicated incoming rain, yet that rain never came. The rain was never promised; the weather forecast only was an educated guess.

"I understand that," the woman said, "being cooped up can make you crazy. Crazy enough to do things like take a dip in the lake when it's cold and cloudy. Haven't you heard the legend about the lake?"

"What legend, ma'am?" Nevaeh asked. "This is my first time even seeing that lake."

"Well, you've gotta go out of your way to find it." The woman reminded her. "You said you're a schoolkid. The programs around here certainly know how to keep you kids busy, if not all the shops. And it's a good thing, or you'd all be trying to jump in that lake."

"Well, as wonderful as they all are, it can get a little monotonous." Nevaeh said.

"Monotonous or safe?" The woman asked her. "You've really never heard of the lake nymph?"

At this moment, Nevaeh's brows raised. Had this woman met the nymph as well, or had she heard some cautionary tale that someone spun up?

"They say she'll get her hands on you and take you all the way to the bottom of the lake to do her bidding." The woman said, speaking in a tone clearly meant to scare children.

Nevaeh, being too old to be fooled by something meant to terrify naive children, scoffed at this idea. "Who told you that? That isn't true."

"No?" The woman asked, her brow raising suspiciously.

"No, not at all." Nevaeh told her. "I met the nymph. She's quite lovely, and she brought me back to the surface."

The woman began to laugh, stirring the tomato soup and filling the air with its aroma. "Maybe you did know that one after all. I try to scare the kids, but I should've figured… High schooler?"

"Well, yes, I am a high schooler, but I was telling the truth." Nevaeh said.

"That swim must have done a number on you." The woman insisted. "Now you're talking nonsense. That tale is just a tall tale to scare the young ones into listening to their elders."

"Well, maybe the tale has *some* truth to it, but the nymph is no monster." Nevaeh said. "She made sure I could breathe underwater, and she showed me the bottom of the lake."

"That's cute," the woman said, speaking as if she were musing to herself, "you haven't lost that sense of wonder. You should write a story, you know. Maybe for the children."

Nevaeh couldn't believe this distant neighbor of hers made such an effort to deny her experience. Though she supposed she couldn't blame her, either; would she herself believe someone else detailing their adventure with a lake nymph? Already, she herself couldn't believe that she could breathe while she was at the bottom of a lake. At this point, she decided it was best to stop trying to convince her neighbor of her experiences; she might only make this kind woman think that she was mad, or that she had been underwater for too long.

"Have you ever noticed the rocks in the lake?" Nevaeh asked.

"Yes, I've seen many lakes with rocks in them." The woman said, adding basil to the soup. "What about the rocks?"

"I just find their formations lovely." Nevaeh said. "The patterns in them, not to mention the plants growing around the lake. It looks… Mystical, or magical. Sublime, even."

The neighbor only became all the more amused. "Is that so? It must be the perfect home for a lake nymph, then. Maybe that's why they made up those stories about that lake."

"It was a nice break from everything else." The girl said. "Everything just began to feel mundane after a while, like clockwork."

"You just need something different every once in a while." The neighbor finished cooking the soup, pouring it into a couple of bowls. "Do you like sandwiches with soup?"

"Oh, if it isn't too much trouble, ma'am." Nevaeh answered.

"Nonsense, I like cooking," she said as she stood to make sandwiches, "and your shoes needed more time to dry anyway."

Nevaeh paid little mind to her clothes still feeling damp, but they certainly had begun to dry. Thankfully, the towels had soaked up some of the moisture. The heater that her neighbor turned on and faced toward her would certainly help to speed that process up; perhaps she would have to pay this woman another visit sometime. She looked around, trying to gauge if she was here by herself. The house had a certain emptiness to it, and it concerned Nevaeh as to if this woman was lonely, or if she was simply alone for the time being. Additionally, it reminded her of the lake nymph who brought her to the bottom of the lake; she only saw fish swimming about.

"There were fish in the lake as well." Nevaeh recounted.

"I prefer fish in the sea." Her neighbor said. "Better for cooking. Bigger."

"That's a fair point." Nevaeh said. "These ones were nice to look at, though."

“Nice to look at, nothing much else to them.” The neighbor replied.

“But do you take time to enjoy nature?” Nevaeh asked. “There’s a reason it inspires art and literature.”

“I’m well aware.” The woman said. “Did seeing it inspire you?”

“I think it did.” Nevaeh said. “I have a surge of energy that I didn’t before. As much as I’ve tried to pace myself and take breaks from school, there’s nothing like getting to go and see the lake.”

“I can relate to that.” The neighbor said with a smile, then bringing the sandwiches she prepared to the table; one for her, and one for her guest. “I used to go with friends on hikes, and my husband used to take me for picnics at the beach.”

“The beach?” Nevaeh repeated. “You better be careful. Haven’t you heard of the ocean nymph? She’s known to take couples to the bottom of the sea.”

The woman busted up laughing, earning a smile from Nevaeh. “You’re quick.” She remarked, dipping her sandwich into her soup. She kept the sandwiches relatively simple, having made grilled cheese and having put apple slices on the sandwich. The tomato soup, however, had not only been seasoned with basil, but also oregano. “Do you want anything else for the soup?”

“No, no. It’s perfect as is.” Nevaeh answered, dunking her sandwich into her soup as well.

“Well, try it first before you decide that.” The woman said.

Nevaeh did as she was told, taking a bite of the sandwich. She chewed with a pensive look on her face, then swallowed. “Like I said. It’s perfect.”

“I like that combination too.” The woman said. “I know I was talking about fish, but we’re out and I wanted something simple. I hope you don’t mind.”

“Not at all. I don’t think I could eat fish after seeing the pretty ones that I saw.” Nevaeh answered honestly. “Thank you for having me over and giving me food. I don’t believe I’ve seen you much, but I should have introduced myself before you brought me here.”

“Not a lot of people know me.” The woman shrugged. “I keep to myself, anyhow. It’s hard work, maintaining a house. But like you said, you need a break from the same exact routine every day.”

“How often do you go to the lake?” Nevaeh asked. “It was so coincidental for you to find me.” She also found it coincidental to stumble upon the lake nymph, but she decided that she would not press the matter; she could prove that she witnessed the glory nature had to offer, yet she could not as easily prove the existence of the entity.

"Well, I don't usually go, but I've been before," she stood to pour a cup of coffee, "and I used to have my kids swim in the summer. I just couldn't believe I saw you sleeping next to the lake."

"So you didn't see me get out of the water?" Nevaeh asked.

"You were already out." The woman said before mixing creamer into her coffee. "Must have been a workout. Would you like some coffee?"

"Oh, sure." Nevaeh said, then noticing a clock on the wall. It had been four hours since she left the house, but as light shined into the house, she realized that the sky was now entirely clear. The notion of her parents wondering where she might be escaped her. However, she was safe and she was being fed. Regardless, she knew she would inevitably have to wash the lake water off of her. Something about the water felt rejuvenating to her, and fortunately, this rejuvenation soaked into her bones and it would not be washed off easily.

"Do you drink coffee with creamer?" The woman asked.

"Yes, thank you." Nevaeh said. "My name is Nevaeh."

"Pleasure to meet you," the neighbor said as she turned around to set the coffee cup before her. "I'm Olivia."

Nevaeh sipped her coffee, assuming that hers was prepared the same way Olivia's was. She enjoyed it, as it was sweetened to her liking. As the sun shone, she warmed up all the more, entirely unbothered by the remaining moisture in her clothes. It was difficult to tell whether or not that warmth also came from her newfound motivation, or from the generosity she was shown.

"I'd hate to cut our visit short, but I should get back to my house." Nevaeh said.

"That's no problem, honey." Olivia replied. "I'll walk you home. Take your time."

When Nevaeh finished her food and her coffee, she stood to retrieve her shoes, handing the towels over to her gracious host. She put the shoes on once she was outside.

"I don't know what your parents will say when they see that you were swimming." Olivia told her. "The sun is out now, so you should dry off a little more on the way."

"That's alright." Nevaeh said. "I'll tell them it was the lake nymph."

Olivia laughed, shaking her head to herself. "You'll have to come by sometime, when my kids are visiting. They studied the sort of things you were talking about today, and I think you'd get along with them."

Recital of Roses

In our village, flowers were integral to our culture. For the flowers to do well often implied that our harvest of crops would be bountiful. As a result, we held a festival every year which commemorated the different flowers growing. Our performers were spectacular, though they were selected at random and prepared for the recital promptly. Not only were they entrusted with performing, but also with putting forth a pleasing enough performance which would make the flowers want to bloom. On the rare occasion that our festivals were dull, it showed in our harvest for the autumn. There were no excuses and no expenses spared; the people were at risk of starvation should we fail to disappoint. Art was the essence of life, and anyone who wanted to live here would learn quickly that we heavily upheld this value, especially if they were to observe our customs.

A selection process was held for the festival, prior to the preparations taking place. Girls were chosen to represent the array of flowers which bloomed in our village. I had always looked up to the girls who got chosen to perform. There was respect for the pressure they were to endure, yet they were always so bright and lively, making it all look fun in spite of the strict organization I could only imagine that followed the selection. Everyone gathered, awaiting the lottery which would bestow the honored roles upon the selected. Members of the community wished they could offer up their daughters or granddaughters; this was no opportunity to miss. In order to keep things fair, nobody could be volunteered by others; every year, one was selected at random. The flowers, as they were called, were young women who were called to represent each flower in our festival and our recital for the year.

There was special prestige, however, that came with the roses; our village incorporated the roses into everything, considering their symbolism for passion and beauty. Passion and beauty drove us, and if you were to ask around, some would say it was the essence of life. Not to mention the quality of our roses; we were sought out specifically for them, and they made us the most money when it came to exporting goods. The flowers we grew were vibrant and colorful, but the roses were especially spectacular and attention grabbing. It showed with the girls selected as the Rose for the festival, namely in how they were done up for the show. Their dresses were always, by far, the most extravagant and called the most attention to them. Each year, it was a challenge to see how the previous year could be outdone.

To be chosen as any of the flowers was a privilege, despite the task being quite daunting. I never imagined that I would be chosen; there were plenty of others in our village who could be chosen. As a child, I aspired to and dreamed of sitting in the seat of one of the flowers, *especially* a Rose. However, as I have matured, I took the weight of the role into consideration, feeling all the more hesitant about wishing to be selected from our lottery system for it. The wisdom which came with age caused me to see those desires to be chosen for the festival as childish dreams. Not that anything was inherently wrong with that; it felt good to dream and to imagine one's potential. It became prominent that this was a childish dream when I overheard the younger children wishing to be one of the flowers.

To be that young once more, to be so carefree that the world seemed so much simpler. This was what I yearned for, considering that adolescents still were treated as children yet expected to begin shouldering responsibility. I envied the joy of the children, the budding blossoms of the village, because it was so simple to please them and their worldview was pure and simple. To think that being one of the flowers, especially the *Rose,* would complete my life, was a youth I wished to reclaim. Life experience lowered self esteem and brought forth complications nobody could expect to arise. I also envied the adults, who also faced life experience and learned to shoulder responsibility. I envied the way they appeared to know what to do, the way they could navigate problems and not allow the falling through of their dreams to effectively destroy them. Plenty of these adults had these same wishes as children, yet many never got to perform as one of the flowers.

The selection process began once again for the year. The Rose selected from last year sat primly in her seat, her hands sitting in her lap as she waited to symbolically pass a rose on to the next girl to be selected. I felt fairly certain her name was Lindsey, but she was known as our current Rose well after the performance and the festival were over. Our previous year's harvest was bountiful, and this was largely accredited to the performance that she prepared. Her delicate movements representing the bloom of the roses dazzled the audience before her, which in and of itself was an immense feat due to our village's obsession with art and beauty. Most could say that we learn creative critique early on, and this added pressure to the performers each year, as they sought to outdo the previous year.

"Welcome to our next annual Flower Fest!" The mayor spoke into the microphone, instantly earning the attention of the attentive audience. "We will be selecting the flowers for this year's performance. Girls ranging between fifteen to twenty five years of age are eligible to be selected by lottery."

Of course, the rules were only explained once more for formality's sake. We knew them by heart by this point, but there always was some chance that someone in the audience could have traveled specifically to see our festival and actually knew nothing of our traditions. Not to mention, some members of the audience could have been too young to show up until this year. Even if they were young, they had many years to learn what we did each year to ensure a good harvest. I found that most children were able to recite the rules of the selection by the time they were around six. I, in particular, had it memorized at around the tender age of five.

"We will start with our Lily." The mayor announced as he reached into the box, shuffling his hand amidst the pieces of paper to manifest anticipation from the audience. Once he finally pulled the little piece of paper from the box, he dramatically raised his hand into the air, then looking over the piece of paper. It was as if he did so to maintain a bravado and to entertain us. "This year's Lily is… Callista Chastain!"

Callista rose from her seat, stepping toward the stage to ascend the steps. The previous year's Lily, Frieda, stood from her seat, waiting for Callista to approach. Callista had a flower crown of lilies bestowed upon her, and she stood in front of Frieda, a proud smile on her face. The applause started off lightly; this was only the beginning of the fun. In spite of the mayor's attempts for formalities, such as requesting that the audience hold their applause for the end, it ended the same every year.

Applause filled the atmosphere as the other flowers were called up, the noise level rising. The selection for the Lily, the Dahlia, the Amaryllis, the Violet, the Heather, the Peony, and the Tulip only led up to the selection for the rose, which everyone anticipated the most.

"Emmeline Andersen, as this year's Forget-Me-Not!"

Why, that certainly makes sense. Good for her. I thought to myself, having always perceived Emmeline that way. That was not to say I saw her in a negative light; the forget-me-not flower held specific meanings tied to loyalty and enduring connection. Although she certainly behaved in a way that implied she demanded not to be forgotten, and I noticed that this was a motif with the Forget-Me-Not's performance. To be any of the flowers was an esteemed prestige, yet I was certain that like most girls hoping to get their name pulled, she wanted to take the spotlight as the Rose. I could not blame my classmate for this in the slightest; the Rose was always the envy of the show.

"And finally, as our Rose…" The mayor read aloud, having plucked a piece of paper from the bowl. The entirety of the village stood in silent anticipation as to who the Rose for this year would be; it certainly had everyone's attention. "… Cadence Briar!"

The people surrounding me, my family included, turned to face me and immediately began to applaud me. I found myself dumbstruck, wondering if I truly was up to the task. However, the stage awaited me, and I obeyed the obligatory motions I was going through, struggling to process the fact that I actually was chosen. The applause began to blur as I made my way to the stage, ascending the steps and standing beside the previous year's Rose. I did not recognize my own steps, nor did I feel each one; I was weightless. I may as well have been carried there, with my entire village applauding me. The now former Rose handed the rose over to me, effectively passing the baton which took the form of a freshly pruned and picked rose.

"Let's give another round of applause for this year's flowers!" The mayor announced, the applause as deafening as ever.

Just as quickly, we were whisked away backstage. I could only imagine for so long what preparation for the festival entailed, but now I got to see it firsthand. I stood alongside the other flowers, and the previous flowers stood behind us. We stood with the gifts bestowed upon us; surely we would have to come up with our own gifts to offer for next year's Flower Fest.

"You all have been chosen as this year's flowers," the mayor explained. "An honor, as I am sure you all have learned over the years. As your predecessors can attest, there is a responsibility that you young ladies must uphold in performing for the Flower Fest. The flowers you are representing each have a part to play in our ritual to ensure our harvest goes smoothly and that we all continue to flourish. You will be thoroughly prepared by the time we have our performance; our time may be limited, but I believe in all of you."

The faith our benevolent mayor placed in us proved overwhelming. I could not readily see how the other girls felt about this, or if there was a difference in the pressure that we felt because I was the Rose. I did not see myself as better than any of them; if anything, I wondered if I truly deserved this privilege altogether. They all looked so ready to take on this honor and to put forth the best performance possible. I enjoyed dancing, but I could not say that I was necessarily the best at it. Normally, hobbies were not about being the best, but my participation in this performance was crucial, and furthermore my skill level.

"Cadence, was it?" The previous Rose said, catching my attention. "I wish you good luck on your performance. Don't overthink it; you'll do great."

Don't overthink it? That's all I can *do.* I thought, wondering if it was a meager attempt to destress me beforehand. Then again, there might have been a method to such madness; stress more than likely would affect a performance. I hoped that dancing could dispel the stress from me, yet it sounded silly and unrealistic. Something my younger self could have been convinced of by a relative.

"Thank you." I said in response. "I will try my best."

"There's no trying; only doing." The previous Rose said. "And you will do wonderfully. I am here for you, and you'll have trainers and collaborators here to help you. This is an exciting honor bestowed upon you; enjoy it while you can. There will be parades, and I encourage you to show up for every single one."

I knew of one parade in particular for the Flower Fest. Over the course of the year, there were other parades held, regardless of the outcome of our performance. The flowers were still honored and revered by the entire village. However, I would not want to be in the place of the Rose the year the harvest was anything but abundant; there was a begrudging respect, in which she was selected for the title of the Rose and was owed her due respect for her position, yet the people did not feel she deserved it given the results. Thankfully, the Rose prior to me was excellent in her performance and often went out of her way to engage with the people. Somebody like her would be vital to look to for advice, yet I hoped she would give me more.

I watched as the other flowers immediately began to prepare a dance for the performance, and to ask for the input of their predecessors. I stood still, wondering what precisely I should be doing and only observing as they set to work immediately. I had to have been the most inadequate Rose that there ever was; they all practiced, and tirelessly might I add. Although they were met with critiques, they fully intended to please with their individual performances.

We were set to meet with fashion designers the next day in order to discuss measurements and what dresses we would wear. I found myself excited for this; the dresses were one of the most enjoyable things about our tradition. Fashion, of course, was an art form that was well respected, just as dance and music were. Our dances would be paired with music, and we would coordinate with the musicians as to how the recital should be conducted. Each flower had a chance to meet with a stylist and to discuss the dress. I eagerly looked forward to how the dress might come to life. Every dress prepared for the festival that I ever laid eyes on were made as if it were the designer's final masterpiece, as if they sought to finish their piece in case it ended as their legacy. The designers did not disappoint in the slightest; every dress was a work of art, and I could not blame the flowers who held onto their dresses well after their duty was fulfilled.

It became increasingly easier to see the others as their roles, even if I grew up with or around some of them. Upon entering the room, the opulence in particular stood out to me, the cushions on the seats embroidered with various flowers. The walls were a deep red, and the light focused primarily on the designer and his sketchpad, as well as the seat presumably meant for the flowers to sit in across from him. Already, I felt cozy, despite the clinical nature of this meeting that I anticipated. "Tell me, how has it been, having been selected? Bragging rights and all."

"It's an honor." I answered simply. I mentally cursed myself for the way my voice wavered; as much of a prestige as it was, it was also nerve wracking.

"That is no way for a Rose to be," he chided lightheartedly. "A Rose is meant to be *bold!* You are our village's proud and *beautiful* symbol."

I eyed the sketchbook before him. The pencil hovered just over the page, ready to draw or to take notes at a moment's notice.

"In several days, you are to take the stage for the big finale." He said, his flamboyant demeanor extinguishing to a serious one. As gaudy and colorful as he and his workspace were, there was no mistake; he was not frivolous in the slightest. "Have you begun to practice your dance?"

"I'm still in the process of organizing my dance." I answered matter-of-factly; it was indeed a work in progress. "There's plenty I have to coordinate with, and you are one of them."

"Excellent answer." The designer commented, starting to draw what looked like a large ball gown. It was a classic choice for the Rose, considering the layers of petals surrounding it. Likewise, layers of fabric would surround the representative. "Mobility has been an issue in the past, although we upgrade every year and do better than the last."

The conversation itself appeared to give the drawing in the sketchbook life. I kept watching with unending fascination, contemplating his process in all of this. Perhaps he evaluated me by talking to me, and this was his way of deciding what was best based on our interaction. The pencil danced, causing me to consider the choreography for when I took the stage.

"By the way," I interjected, my gaze shifting to his concentrated expression, "what's your name?"

This caused him to stop; he must not have been asked about himself before. He met with different girls every year, and I figured he was used to making different dresses for them over the years. I wondered if former flowers came to visit him; he deserved his proper acknowledgement in preparing us, after all.

"My name is Dominic." He answered. There seemed to be a sort of admiration in his gaze; something I did earned his respect. Had nobody bothered to ask his name before?

"It's nice to meet you." I said. "My name is Cadence."

"A pleasure to meet you." Dominic responded. "As nice as it is to speak plainly, I and everyone else will see you as the Rose, and will refer to you as such until you've passed your role onto another."

"Why is that? Why do we refer to the girls by their flower names?" I questioned. "It's only a role, is it not?"

"Why, yes it is." Dominic answered. "But it's a special role that many of our fellow villagers don't have the privilege of ever taking up, no matter how hard they wish for it."

"I understand that," I said, "but why the insistence on referring to us by our titles? We all are so different."

"As are literal flowers, my dear," he explained, "but all the same, they are categorized. A rose could be pink or red or white, but it is a rose all the same. As for myself, I choose to call the flowers by their names because it makes life simpler for me; just as they have their role to play, I do too. I am merely the designer for the show."

"But that isn't all you are." I argued. "You make the show come to life, there has to be an interesting story behind how you got here."

"I'm sure there's an interesting story as to how *you* got here." Dominic smiled, as if amused by my persistence in wanting to connect beyond our roles in this festival.

"It's the same as any other, and it just may bore you." I shrugged.

That day really was like any other selection day. I, like the others, hoped to be chosen. Even as I recognized the weight of the responsibility, I still undeniably yearned for it, even when I wondered whether or not I could actually inspire others as the Rose. However, I found myself considering the idea that fate itself allowed me into this position, and by divine intervention, that would mean that I *was* suited to the role. I also found it silly; other girls all were selected all the same, in the same exact manner. If I were selected because fate ordained it, then that would mean all of them were too, even those who failed to live up to the task.

The days blurred together; it all progressed way too fast. The parade was where I debuted in my dress designed by Dominic; it appeared our conversation truly inspired him, as the gown resembled what a princess in a fairy tale would wear. A princess of roses could easily be envisioned in this outfit, and here I was with the honor of wearing it. The gown was a deep red, although roses and rosettes of varying colors were fixed into the dress. These roses were kept as buds when the dress was presented to me, but they were allowed to start growing and blossoming so that they would bloom by the time the day of the festival arrived. Thankfully, there were no thorns in this design; there had been years where it was used as a disciplinary measure to ensure the Rose had a proper posture.

"Oh, no sweetie." I stopped a child from attempting to pick the roses off of my dress, figuring my light warning would be better than a full blown scolding from an adult. "… If you're good, I'll be sure to toss a rose out to you when I spot you in the audience at the recital."

This was good enough for the child, who smiled and ran off to be part of the crowd. I was handed a bouquet of roses, and my peers were handed bouquets of their respective flowers. We all had the option of keeping the bouquet to ourselves and potentially gifting it to someone, such as family, friends, or even a romantic partner, or to toss individual flowers out to the crowd as our carts rolled by. Most often, the flowers opted for the latter, seeing as it was an easy way to become an unrecognizable fan favorite. I, too, would choose this option. There always was ample opportunity to find more roses in this village, especially if the performance went well.

After the parade, I was off to practice one last time. Practice, practice, practice. Given that my trainer was a perfectionist assigned to the Rose, I did not blame her for her strictness. While she endured immense pressure placed upon her shoulders, I shouldered the heaviest burden: to carry out the performance which would be judged by all. I wanted breaks. Eventually, she caved and allowed me one for a mere five minutes. I sat down, and Lindsey placed a foot stool in front of me to prop my feet up. I sighed and reached for the water that was provided. "To think that this experience is so magical…"

"Now, that isn't a complaint, is it?" Lindsey chided. "A great honor has been bestowed upon you."

"Yes, and it's a task I must live up to." I responded. "It's been days since I've seen my family."

"I know how that is." She sympathized. "It'll only make them all the more grateful for you to come home after the recital."

I remembered that there was a point after the performance was over that the flowers would return to the families that they lived with, who eagerly awaited their return after their cultivation for the festival. Cameras would showcase them, when it used to only be a spotlight following each of them. There was magic within that spotlight; many of the children in the village believed it was magic, rather than the lighting ordered specifically to follow them. Additionally, there was a sparkly, shimmery dust which fell over the flowers afterwards. The amount of shimmering meant that the flowers fulfilled their duty, as well as how abundant the harvest would be for that year. I listened to the conversations taking place between my peers in school, that it clearly was based off of the ranking that the audience gave, that the whole idea of the performance connecting to the harvest was a sham.

The idea of our tradition being for nothing was a deep rooted fear of mine; was I expected to keep a farce up for the sake of the children? Already, there were so many lies we told children. Furthermore, the idea that anyone in charge could stage this and use it as an excuse as to whether or not our village thrived with abundant harvests filled me with dread like no other. The adults in our village also all believed so ardently in this, as if they would be insulted if you were to dare question it.

"I might need a longer break." I told Lindsey.

"Are you alright?" Lindsey asked, concern furrowing in her brows.

"Yeah, I just haven't eaten much today." I answered.

"*Haven't eaten much?*" A different voice echoed from behind us. "Unacceptable. Food gives you the fuel that you need to dance!"

We turned to face the source of the voice. The Heather from the previous year; surely this meant that the current Heather was up to perform. If I remember correctly, the previous one's name was Heather. A happy coincidence that she was chosen as a flower she shared a name with.

"I was just trying not to stuff myself." I put my hand up defensively.

"Refraining from food is a problem, and I insist you do something about that." She briskly walked away to prepare a plate from the refreshments table before I could stop her. Upon returning, she provided me with quick snacks that could be eaten before my performance, such as succulent watermelon, a granola bar, some yogurt, and a bottle of water. “I don’t want to see you on your feet until you’ve eaten.”

“Thank you.” I said, deciding against questioning her authority or attempting to turn her down. My rumbling belly would have punished me for it.

“No, thank *you* for your service as the Rose.” She said, pulling another chair up. “Lindsey, you’ve been on your feet all day. Take a seat, won’t you?”

As obliged, Lindsey sat down gracefully. It was something she and my trainer worked on with me, to ensure that I maintained the graceful posture expected of the Rose. Each time I was scolded for plopping down onto furniture as I pleased, Lindsey cringed, as if reminded of her own training.

“All of the preparations for the Flower Fest are exhausting. It’s important to nourish yourself and rest properly.” Heather said. “You also need to have fun. Honestly, how do they expect a dazzling performance if they let their flowers wilt?”

I nodded in agreement with her as I ate. Of course, I felt no pressure to speak; it was rude to speak with one’s mouth full. Perhaps this was what she intended.

"You've been doing well up to this point." She said, having pulled up her own chair so she could sit amongst us. Granted, she was an authority and could assert herself as such, but she proved humble enough to sit with us rather than to stand over us. A virtue I believed all of the flowers should embody. "Many think that a Rose should be haughty, because of all the attention and because of the role they play in the village. But the best Roses that I've seen make the effort to connect with the people, and to give to others. That's the role of the flower itself, you know; a lot of people think it's simply to look pretty and to be offered up as gifts, but roses show signs that there's sustenance in the area they grow in. In fact, that's how our village was founded in the first place! Because the founders found roses, and that showed that we have a water source, healthy soil for crops to grow, good weather for us all to survive…"

"That, in and of itself, sounds like magic." I remarked once I had the chance, before taking another bite of the food I was offered.

"It does!" Heather said. "And to think that this all revolves around natural order and human instinct. It's amazing what people know how to look for in order to survive."

“Forgive me, but I’ve heard rumors that some of the villagers don’t believe it has to do with anything magical.” I said. “That it’s because of the people in charge, like the mayor and the people who work with him.”

“Please,” she scoffed, “do you *really* think the mayor is capable of all that on his own? Even if he collaborates with others. I couldn’t tell you where the shimmering dust comes from, but I have only ever known it to mean approval of the performance, and that we’re getting our crops.”

I couldn’t help but to grin, amused by her matter-of-fact demeanor. I listened attentively, trying to gauge which flower was performing as a means of understanding when I would be next. Earlier that day, we discussed when each flower was to come out to dance. I was listed for the last dance for the recital as the Rose, just after the Dahlia. I heard the Forget-Me-Not’s music, recognizing it from hearing the music at rehearsals. When I peeked, I realized Emmeline was wrapping her performance up, taking a bow. Her dress was stunning, a shorter dress that allowed for easier movement with forget-me-not flowers fixed onto it. She retreated backstage as the next flower was announced.

"Let's give it up one more time for our Forget-Me-Not!" The mayor proclaimed, resulting in applause for her. "Next up, we have the Dance of Dahlias!"

It alarmed me that already, I was almost up. The Dahlia, a young woman by the name of Daisy, conducted herself with such grace in her large pink dress. I thought my dress was heavy, but hers was designed to represent how bushy dahlias were. I found myself practically mesmerized by the twirls, hoping that I, too, could achieve that same level of grace.

"Not getting nervous, are you?" Heather asked me, then taking the trash from the food she brought for me. "You've been working so hard; you're ready."

"They're all doing so wonderfully out there." I commented.

"As will you!" She replied. "You all have been working hard for this night. You deserve the right to relish in the spotlight and to enjoy yourself."

"Let's give it up for our Dahlia!" The mayor announced, the applause sounding once more. "And for our big finale… The Recital of Roses!"

The names of the dances changed each year, and this year the flowers went with an alliteration theme. The Tulip, for instance, performed a Tulip Tango. I stepped out onto the stage, welcomed by the continued applause which eventually silenced so I could perform. The roses on my dress were in full bloom, timed appropriately for the evening. My dress swished across the stage, having trailblazed a clear path amidst the petals from the other flowers' dances. As the orchestra started to perform the sonata, I began to move with the rhythm, just as rehearsed. The lights made it more difficult to look into the faces of the crowd, though I could tell they waited in eager anticipation to watch the performance I prepared.

I sidestepped, starting with a basic twirl. The music started slow, as did each movement. The beginning of the dance was practiced to perfection; I was certain I could do it in my sleep. As the tempo picked up, my twirling did as well. This was where I struggled during practice; my trainer often scolded me, as I tended to trip when it sped up. So far, so good; I was doing even better managing the folk dance than I originally expected! The audience prematurely began to cheer, and euphoria rose within me. And then, it happened.

I slipped.

Gasps erupted from the audience. Within that moment, I could easily picture my trainer wincing, the shame I might bring should I allow myself to clumsily fall to the floor. Thankfully, I caught myself with a klutzy side step, though I managed to divert the attention away from this by taking several of the roses off of my dress and tossing them into the crowd. Just then, I recognized the child from the parade, smiling while catching one of the roses. From there, I managed to continue the dance, as if nothing happened. I earned more excited shouts and cheers, and I was unable to keep the smile off my face. I embodied the Rose, in spite of the slip-up. In the back of my mind, I concerned myself as to how that might affect my performance and the harvest for this year, yet I had no time to focus on this and only to continue dancing until the music stopped. In between twirls, I tossed more roses into the crowd. The dress swished, and more petals were swept to the side to make room for me. The dance ended with me twirling back to the center of the stage and stopping before lifting the sides of the skirt and bowing. The audience's reaction proved encouraging; perhaps I smoothly played off the mistake I made.

"One more time, for the Rose!" The mayor announced, the cheers growing deafening. The other flowers came back out from backstage, and they stood around me. I extended my hands to the two by my sides, the Amaryllis and the Heather. Once they held my hands, the other flowers beside them held their hands, and so on and so forth until we all held hands, then we lifted our hands into the air proudly. Internally, I worried; I was grateful for the support from not only the audience but also my fellow flowers. I had yet to see the familiar shimmering, hoping I did not ruin everything. But just as doubt crept in, hope was recovered; the gold, shimmering dust sprinkled all over every single flower, coating us in it as the audience became louder than before. We were effectively relieved of our duty in performing for the sake of the harvest; it would be abundant this year.

Forest of Fantasy

People never knew of the existence of fairies. Perhaps, for the sake of the fairies, we should keep it that way. Human beings *are* pretty dangerous, you know.

I lived in a house surrounded by a forest with my family. A small, simple family, but still a perfectly loving family. The forest looked exactly like the setting of a fairy tale. Leaves did not fall from the trees; they danced down from them. The flowers were not pretty or beautiful; they were gorgeous and extravagant. There was space for me to run around and play and pretend I was living in a fairy tale.

My parents noticed my childish passion for fairy tales and took pleasure in watching me play happily. It was as if my life were the Happily Ever After of a fairy tale. My mother was the princess who was saved by my father, the knight in shining armor, and they got married and later had my brother Mike and me. Together, we made the Harris family.

As a young girl of five years, I had quite the imagination. I inherited this sense of wonder from my mother, a bright and cheerful woman who I also gained most of my appearance from. She always told me fairy tales to enhance my imagination and give me jovial, optimistic thoughts. She told me the stories in such a way that made them seem entirely real, giving me the idea that mythical creatures such as fairies or mermaids could actually exist. I was particularly interested in fairies.

There were people, however, who opposed my imagination. My father, for example, a logical, no-nonsense man, would tell me that such creatures did not exist and wanted to clear the idea from my mind. Usually when he told me such things, he said them irritably. I viewed his ideas as pessimistic, while he viewed them as realistic. He was not a grouchy, unloving man however; he doted on me and treated me like a little princess, even building my room to look like a fairy tale room. Sometimes he would encourage my imagination when he was in a happier mood and was glad to see me being a child. He may have supposed that I would grow out of it, amusing my imagination and hoping it would blossom into creativity and productivity. He may have also wanted to cherish moments from my childhood before I had to truly face reality. I recognized, even in my early years, that my mother would tell him to back off and "let her be a kid".

Older children at my elementary school were also pessimistic. They were far too logical, and whenever I entered the school, I felt so much younger than all of them because of my alleged immaturity. "You believe in fairies, Kirsten? That's for babies!", "Fairies aren't real!", "You believe in *fairies*? What are you, three?", and "Kirsten likes little kid stuff!" were all everyday things I would hear from the mouths of the older kids. It was assumed their parents would not put up with their imagination like mine would. I found it sad that parents would not care to see their children be children, like mine would, most of the time.

Sometimes it felt like my father wanted me to act like these kids. My mother, however, always encouraged me to hold on to my imagination, no matter how hard others tried to shake me of it. She believed because they lost their sense of wonder, the world around them became dull, which made them dull. She would read stories to me at night before bed, such as your basic fairy tales like "Cinderella" or "The Little Mermaid". However, she would also tell me stories she made up in a way that made them seem real. I asked her how she was able to make it seem so real one night, and she simply smiled and said "I used my imagination, Kirsten. If you have imagination, anything is possible." Her advice was enchanting to my young mind. It was my motto from then on.

One night, my mother and my father were conversing. I had been awaiting my mother's bedtime story of the night, and I entered the living room to call her into my room.

"Mommy," I whined, "I can't sleep without my bedtime story!"

"Kirsten, not now." Daddy said. "Mommy's busy. Just go to bed."

"But I can't--"

"*Go. To. Bed. Kirsten.*" Daddy said, pointing toward my room. He was not in a good mood that night, for he usually would have more patience with me.

I obeyed my father's curt command to go to bed. My bedroom was designed to be like a fairy tale room because of my love for fairy tales and my childish desire to be a princess. I lay in my soft, pink bed, slipping into the thick blankets. My bed was a mushy, fluffy bed, but it was only sturdy enough to support my back and function as a bed rather than a bean bag chair. I hoped that dreamland would hold fantasy for me, as my mother would tell me before I went to sleep. She did not come in to tell me goodnight, as she usually would. I tossed and turned, finding myself unable to sleep without my mother filling my mind with wonderful fantasies.

I heard something outside my window that I had never heard before. *Is this... Fluttering?* I wondered, thinking of my mother's stories and her vivid descriptions of fairies, as though she had actually seen them. The ideas of fairies sounded exhilarating to my young mind, though other people would shoot down my childish imagination and try to persuade me that such creatures are not real. It sounded far too unfair. Wonderful creatures like that simply *must* exist! Yet at the same time, I had to think logically, like the rest of the world, even though my mother wanted me to always cling to my fantasies and imagination as though my life depended on it.

A noise interrupted my thoughts. There was the fluttering again! I looked around the room, slowly and hesitantly standing up, scared my father would walk in and see me out of bed. "Hello?" I called. I opened my window. Seeing something glittering, I jumped out to run after it.

I turned to the right, for I saw the light fly into the forest in that direction. The light was keeping me from panicking due to my fear of the dark. As long as I had some form of a light source, I was okay. I dashed after the light as fast as my short legs could carry me. I felt like I ran a mile out into the forest before I found what I was looking for.

I encountered the light, seemingly all by itself. It floated away from me as if it wanted me to follow. I strode after it obediently, then stepping past some sort of force field. I looked around, and I was standing in a miniature village. I felt like a giant and wondered where the villagers were. The lights within this village were fluorescent and colorful. It felt like I was in a lit up ballroom during the evening, as in "Beauty and the Beast". The light that guided me to this place appeared in front of me, taking the form of a tiny person with bright wings. It was a fairy! It took on feminine features. It was a girl fairy!

"Welcome to our village," the girl fairy said. "Your name is Kirsten, right?"

I nodded, staring at her in astonishment. "You're a fairy," I said, awestruck.

"Why, yes," she giggled, "yes I am. My name is Astoria, and I wanted to show you our village, Kirsten."

Was this really happening? I was meeting a *fairy!* Just like the ones from my bedtime stories. She was pretty and tiny, like Mommy described fairies to be.

"Would you like a tour?" Astoria offered, to which I obviously replied with an enthusiastic nod. "Great! Now, if you'll come wi--"

"Astoria!" another fairy yelled. It was a boy fairy. "Where the hell were you? Everyone was worried sick! We were gonna send a search party after your--"

"Hey hey hey!" Astoria interrupted. "Don't use bad words in front of a little girl."

The boy fairy stared up at my face, his eyes widening in horror. "Little?" he gulped nervously.

"This is Kirsten," Astoria said cheerfully, "she's the one I was talking about!"

I was excited about the idea of fairies talking about me. They had known about me for longer than I thought.

"Oops! Pardon my bad manners, Kirsten," Astoria said. "This is my brother Ignis."

"Astoria!" Ignis said. "You brought a *human* into our village? That is against the fairy law!"

"Pfft. Like you actually follow the rules all the time." Astoria replied sarcastically. I did not know how old she was, but she looked like a teenage fairy. "Besides, I think she can help us. I feel like she is the one, the one who will keep them away from us."

"Keep who away?" I asked.

"Astoria, leaving like that is not okay," Ignis said, completely ignoring me, "and bringing a human into the village? Not even *I* would do that! Plus, how would a little kid keep *them* away?"

"Keep *who* away?" I repeated.

"Oh!" Ignis said. "N-None of your business, kid!"

Astoria rolled her eyes at Ignis. "We can tell her, Ignis. She's the one, I know it."

"Astoria, you trust people too easily," Ignis said. "You have the poorest sense of judgment. Choosing a *kid?* I know you're an airhead and all, but I never thought you'd be this senseless."

"It sure seems to run in the family," she retorted.

"What's going on?" I interrupted, reminding them of my presence. Astoria looked at Ignis, sighed, and pleadingly looked at me.

"Kirsten," she said, "our people have been spotted somewhere outside the village and we have been suspected ever since."

"Yeah, our 'people'," Ignis said. "More like Astoria just *had* to go out and watch humans and was seen by some stupid human."

"Shut it!" Astoria shouted. "I only wished to observe their behavior. Anyway, Kirsten, we need your help."

"What do you need?" I asked.

"She won't be able to do this," Ignis said. "She's a child, Astoria. It was stupid of you to bring her."

"You're a butt," I crossed my arms. Astoria giggled, pointing at Ignis.

"Excuse me?" Ignis raised his eyebrow. "A butt? What kind of insult is that?"

Astoria and I laughed as he flew around me shouting how illogical of a child I was. Ignis seemed to enjoy being a butt to his younger sister, like Mike was to me. I then thought of my brother, turning to face Astoria.

"Can I get my brother?" I requested. Ignis snickered and Astoria gasped.

"Um, Kirsten..." Astoria said. "Humans are not supposed to know about fairies. We need to keep this as secret as we can."

"Mike can keep a secret!" I promised.

"Clearly you can't," Ignis sneered, Astoria elbowing him. "Ow!"

"Very well," she replied, "but only him. No more. Got it?"

"Uh-huh!" I nodded, running off to go home.

I snuck up to my house, creeping to Mike's window silently. I opened it and jumped in. I poked my brother.

"Mike. Mike. Mike." I said. "Wake uuuuuuup."

"... Nnngh. Kirsten?" Mike said. My seven year old brother sat up. "What's going on?"

"It's fairies!" I exclaimed in a hushed voice. He gave me a slow blink as a response.

"Kirsten," he said, "that's little kid stuff. Go to bed." He thought he was much more sophisticated than me because he was two years older than me and he did not believe in fairy tales.

"They're real!" I said, shaking him. "Get up! I'll show you!"

"Okay, okay!" Mike said, sitting up and yawning. "Lead the way."

I jumped out of his window and motioned for him to do the same. He gave me a strange look.

"We're leaving the house?" he asked.

"Yeah," I said. "Come on!"

When Mike jumped out of his window, I grabbed his wrist and practically dragged him to the secret fairy village. We stood in it for a few seconds, not seeing the village.

"Astoria?" I called.

"Astoria? What kind of name is that?" Mike asked. "You had another dream, Kirsten. Mom should really stop telling you those stori--"

The area around us turned into the enchanting village I saw before. Mike was left speechless, regretting anything and everything he ever said about not believing in fairy tales. Astoria flew to me immediately with a crowd behind her.

"Oh good, you're here!" she said. "This is your brother, I take it? The one who doesn't believe in fairies?"

"Uhh..." Mike stammered, his eyes widening in fear.

"I'm just teasing," she giggled. "People aren't supposed to know about us anyway. So you two can consider yourselves pretty lucky."

"Astoria, your judgment is rather..." a girl fairy said. "Questionable."

"Well, maybe her brother could help too!" Astoria said optimistically.

"What's going on? What am I helping with?" Mike asked. "Your name is weird."

"Thanks, so is yours," Astoria replied sarcastically. "And if you must know, we were seen by a human. This human is a hunter, and now he wants to find us and... And he..."

"And he wants to ki-- Ow! Astoria!" Ignis rubbed his arm, which suffered another elbow from Astoria.

"You don't just say that in front of little kids!" Astoria shouted.

"They're old enough to understand what dy-- Ow! Stop that!"

"Disappearing. He means disappearing." Astoria said, covering up "dying". I did understand the concept of dying, for some of my relatives had died. "We will disappear if the hunter finds us. We need your help, Kirsten. We need to figure out a way to live in peace without humans interfering."

"Humans *are* interfering," a boy fairy said.

"They're here to help," Astoria glared. "It was my fault, so I decided to right my wrong."

"What do I need to do?" I asked.

"You need to keep them away from us," she said. "We'll try to think of something. We overheard humans talking about hunting for fairies, and we need to convince them that we don't exist."

"Why don't we give the poor girl a tour of our village first?" an authoritative girl fairy said. Astoria gasped when she saw who the fairy was.

"Laurea! How did you--"

"Ignis filled me in," Laurea said, "and a leader must know what occurs in her village. You brought a human into our village?"

"W-Well, I wanted to--"

"Astoria, I want a straight answer. I did not ask for your explanation just yet."

"... Yes. I brought two humans. This girl and her older brother."

"Very well. Why did you bring them?"

"I wanted to find help in order to right my wrong," Astoria said.

"Ah," Laurea said, flying up to my face to observe me. "Interesting. She's still in the stage where humans are pure of heart. She has yet to be corrupt, like most humans. Welcome to our village, Kirsten Harris."

"Thank you," I said.

"Astoria will give you a tour of the village," Laurea said, Astoria obeying her. We then heard noise off in the distance.

"Oh no," Astoria said. "We didn't come up with a plan."

"Hey, you could come up with a plan, right?" Ignis asked. I nodded.

"Go, Kirsten," Astoria said. "You must stop the hunters. We don't want to... Disappear."

I nodded, accepting my duty to protect the mystical creatures. I did not know these hunters, but I was more than ready to stop them from finding the fairies. Our plan was perfected, and all we needed to do was put it to action without any mishaps. Still, I was nervous, for I had the most difficult task in the entire plan.

I watched as the fairies were shutting their secret village down and getting Mike to follow them to a hiding spot. The light faded from my surroundings, giving the forest an ominous feel rather than a magical one. While I was hidden by the pitch black darkness, I felt a horrifying sense of danger around me. I could not mess this up now; I had to lead the hunters away from both the fairies and the mere idea of them. But I couldn't help but feel absolutely *terrified!* I was tempted to cry and I wanted my mother, but

I had to be brave. I was going to stop adults -- grown men, to be exact -- from getting what they wanted. If that did not take guts, I did not know what did.

I remembered the small flashlight in my pocket. I whipped it out and turned it on, feeling safer than before. I looked around for the hunters, and then heard a noise somewhere to the right. I turned in that direction and advanced forward, the source of the noise growing closer. The sound became clearer and clearer the closer I came; I was able to recognize it as men's voices. The source of the noise was still far from me, and fortunately I remembered the plan. I thought of possible distractions, rushing my brain to force out an idea. My eyes widened as I came up with a distraction. I started running around with my flashlight as though I were playing. I laughed delightedly.

"Hey, what was that?" a man's voice said.

"Let's press on," a more familiar voice said. "We might find those fairies you were talking about, Marty."

I continued to run around and play. Footsteps were heard coming closer and closer. The closer they became, the more I could see them. Some had their guns raised in case they found something.

"There's a light!" Marty yelled. "The fairies! I knew it! Right the--"

"Lower your guns!" one of the hunters, whom I recognized as my father, ordered. "That's my little girl."

They stared at me as I finally stopped running around and stared back at them. Daddy approached me.

"Kirsten," he said, surprised, "what are you doing? You should be at home and in bed."

"It was me all along," I lied.

"What was you all along, Kirsten?" Daddy asked in a demanding tone.

"The fairy stuff," I said, making it up as I went along. "It was all me. Playing pretend!"

"What about those lights I saw?" Marty said. I flashed my flashlight at him as a response.

"And those noises," another hunter commented. "What was that?"

"It was me," I said, screeching and imitating the fluttering sounds the fairies made when they flew. "See? I got you! I got you all! Fairies..." I felt uncomfortable just *saying* the next part. "Just like you say, Daddy... Fairies are not even real."

I tried to hide my sadness from them. My father sighed, disappointed that he and his friends had been fooled. They looked at each other, unsure of what to do next.

"I guess we could just head home," one of the hunters suggested. Daddy remained while they all left.

"Kirsten," he said, "why would you pull such a prank? Do you realize that something could've happened to you? You could've been hurt. Your mother must be worried sick."

"I'm sorry, Daddy." I said sadly. "I wanted to mess with you guys."

"Kirsten, I should punish you for leaving the house at night like that," he said, "but I'm just glad you're okay." He dropped to his knees and hugged me tightly. "Now we've gotta get home."

"Okay Daddy," I said, smiling. "I'm gonna go the way that I came. I'll see you at home."

"Are you sure you won't get lost?" he asked.

"I won't," I replied. I would not get lost in this forest because of how well I knew it. I ran in the direction of the fairies, my flashlight in my hand. I needed to find them and see if they were safe. I also needed to bring Mike home with me.

I stopped when I reached their village, looking around. My exhaustion started to take a toll on me. I was then surrounded by lights again; the familiar, mystical lights I was introduced to tonight. The lights surrounding me were then accompanied by friendly, high-pitched voices.

"Kirsten, you did it," Astoria said proudly. "I knew you were the right one."

"Well done, kiddo," Ignis said. "You didn't screw it up."

Astoria smacked him in the back of his head and shook her head at him. They were like Mike and I sometimes.

"We can continue to live here in peace thanks to you, Kirsten," Laurea said. "Thank you for keeping our people safe. We are forever grateful to you for keeping the knowledge of our existence from falling into the wrong hands."

* * *

My eyes opened slowly, allowing me to take in my surroundings; I was in my bedroom. I sat up and looked around. Usually, waking up in this wonderful bedroom would delight me, however it had no such effect today; it seemed too realistic and dull in comparison to what I had seen the previous night.

I rose out of bed like an adult would; sober and exhausted at how the world really was. I was not as cheery as I usually was. What I had seen was not like anything I had seen before. I would share this exhilarating experience with other people, but they would not believe me. And what proof did I have? How did I know that what happened was real? It must have been, for my young mind could not possibly dream something like that up on its own. That was *not* my imagination.

"Kirsten, darling," my mother called, "breakfast is ready!"

I yawned, stretching my arms upwards then lowering them and exiting from my room. When I approached the table, my mother noticed my unusually grim expression.

"Is there anything wrong, Kirsten?" Mom frowned.

"No," I sighed, eating my breakfast. She was sad when I was disillusioned. My father stared out the window, contemplative. I was curious as to what could have been on his mind. He looked at me and exited the room briskly. I frowned at his sudden want to distance himself from us.

"Did Daddy eat breakfast yet?" I asked.

"No," Mom answered, concerned and quickly thinking of something. "How about you go tell him to come eat with us?"

I did as she said and followed Daddy to the other room. I glanced at Mike briefly, wondering if I should bring up the events of the previous night. I was too worried, for he could possibly think I was loony. I turned to my father.

"Daddy," I said. "Mom made breakfast."

"I know, sweetheart." Daddy said somewhat coldly.

"Then why didn't you eat?" I asked.

"... I'm not too hungry this morning, Kirsten." Daddy said.

I left the room sadly. There was nobody I could discuss the fairies with. Mom was not there, Daddy was upset, and Mike could think me silly for still believing in fairies. It could have been a dream after all, and fairies could simply not be real. Why would my mother tell me such sweet lies before I went to sleep? Did she not know that I would one day discover the horrible truth? I thought of her spitefully as a liar and a loon.

Poor Daddy, he looked as though he felt awful. He never told me directly, but he felt disappointed. I was unsure of why exactly. Was it because I was out at night? Was it because he and his friends failed to find the fairies they were looking for? Was it something that occurred when I was not around? I felt horrible seeing him feel so bad, as if he failed to accomplish something.

* * *

I lay down on my bed, glad that the day was finally over. I hated seeing my father depressed, I hated not being able to discuss the fairies I saw with anyone, and I hated the strange, unmagical day I had. I was hoping I would go to sleep quickly. Maybe I would see the fairies again! No matter what I dreamt about, it would definitely be better than what had happened today.

There was a noise outside my window which interrupted my thoughts. Or was it all in my head? The noise was what I believed to be the fluttering. *It isn't real,* I mentally sighed. I tossed and turned in my bed. My memory began returning to me, and I recalled Astoria finally giving me the tour when I returned to the village. I felt a pain in my chest and tears stinging in my eyes as I remembered the fun I had and considered that it was not real. *My fun can never be real now,* I thought. I then recalled meeting more fairies and running around, playfully chasing my fairy friends with Mike. Laurea smiled at us.

"Come back whenever you wish," she said. "You are always welcome in our village, Kirsten. You are our hero."

I heard even more noise outside my window. It was rather distracting, and I finally rose from my bed to see if anything was outside my window. I slowly approached the window, somewhat nervous to see what it was. There was a light source on my window, which confused me, as it was nighttime. I discovered the light source; it was glittering gold letters which sparkled and spelled out "THANK YOU". I smiled and realized I was indeed awake. I thought of when I would see the fairies again and imagined what I would do with them.

www.ingramcontent.com/pod-product-compliance
Lightning Source LLC
Chambersburg PA
CBHW071129100726
47908CB00008B/2542
9798992140101